Iron Cop

by

Sally Booth

Iron Cop

Cover Art by *Diana Carlile*

The Wild Rose Press, Inc.
PO Box 708
Adams Basin, NY 14410-0708
Visit us at www.thewildrosepress.com

Publishing History
First Crimson Rose Edition, 2018
Print ISBN 978-1-5092-2157-8
Digital ISBN 978-1-5092-2158-5

Published in the United States of America

Dedication

Iron Cop is dedicated to my three children,
Deborah, Denise, and Donald,
for all the loving encouragement and support
they have given me
in the many ventures I have undertaken.
I love you and cherish each of you.

Acknowledgments

My appreciation goes to my "Special" daughter, Katherine Ludewig, who willingly struggled through all of my first attempts at writing.

~*~

Thank you to the members, past and present, of the Saratoga Romance Writers of America who helped me to make *Iron Cop* the book it is today.

A special thank you to my friend, Lisette Belisle, who spent many, many hours with me on the telephone brainstorming this book.

I'm grateful to Dorice Nelson who did her best to point out every grammatical mistake I made.

Finally, to my dear departed friend, Ludima Gus Burton, who was a constant in reminding me to "get that book finished."

Prologue

A strange noise woke Samantha Thorne from a sound sleep. Shooting upright, she called to her husband, "Edward? Is that you?" She glanced at the clock. One a.m.

Pop. Pop. Thump.

Edward cried out in pain. Loud voices rose from the foyer.

"What on earth…?" Samantha slipped on her white satin robe and slippers and opened her bedroom door. The voices became even louder and were coming from Edward's study to the left of the front door.

She stepped onto the landing overlooking the foyer. A faint glow came from her husband's study. Who in the world would be visiting at this hour? The tone of their voices caused a weird feeling in her stomach. She took a step toward the stairs when Edward cried out again.

"No. Please don't," he begged.

Samantha stopped and grabbed for the railing. The terror in Edward's voice sent rapid chills through her. Her heartbeat pounded like the hooves of a racehorse bearing down the home stretch. What did they want? What were they doing to him?

Pop. Thump.

Before she could make a move, a big form filled the doorway to Edward's study. A man dressed all in black stepped forward.

Samantha crouched back into the shadows, shaking and praying he hadn't seen her.

The huge man turned on the foyer lights, never taking his gaze from her. His dead silver eyes and deformed face scared the breath out of her. She stood in shock, unable to move. Another man with a shining bald head and a white suit came out of the study and stood beside the giant. The bald man tilted his head toward the giant and mumbled something.

The giant pulled his gun.

Then fired at her.

Chapter 1

One Month Later

Nick O'Reilly stood in the middle of Captain Bianco's office trying to remember if he had ever been this frustrated. "Captain, I'm a detective not a bodyguard."

"I need my best man to guard this witness. She is the only one who can provide the information we need in court to put Chico Vargas in the Clinton Correctional Facility for the rest of his life."

"Don't we have people trained to protect witnesses?" Nick argued.

"Yes, we do. But they aren't you."

"What about the murder case Mike and I are working on? We almost have it wrapped up."

"We've assigned a temporary partner to work with Mike."

Nick sighed. He knew the captain well enough to know his mind was set, and the Almighty Himself would not be changing his mind. "You're the boss, Captain. What do I need to know?"

"Here's the file." He handed a thick folder to Nick and pointed to it, "Everything you need to know is in there. Lock yourself away someplace and read it."

Bodyguard. Hell! He had worked hard to earn the rank of detective. Nick glared at his mentor and captain.

"You really want me for this job?"

"It's an order, son, and it begins ASAP."

That did it. He knew the captain had set him on a mission he hated but knew Nick would do the job and protect this witness to the best of his ability.

Crossing county lines a few minutes later, Nick sat in his car in Albany's Washington Park where he would not be disturbed. He opened the cover. "Wow." Staring back at him was a picture of this gorgeous curly haired strawberry blonde with deep emerald green eyes. What a hottie. Sure, he would do his best to protect this one. Can't let anything happen to a young lady who looks this good. Twenty-seven. Just the right age, too. Hot Miranda rights!

He read further and cursed. Samantha Chadwick-Thorne. A high society dame. Just what he didn't need. He had vowed to never have anything to do with "high society" anything after literally being left at the church altar by one such... Damnation.

Still sputtering and wanting to get to the meat of the case, Nick turned the page to see why he had to protect this beauty. He read muttering out loud as he went. "She was sleeping. Heard something. Got up. Rushed out of bedroom. Heard shots. Victim screaming. Hmm. Torturing victim. Shooting him in knees, arms and heart. Vargas and sidekick spot the wife. Shoot her in the arm. Wow. She got shot. She escapes. Passageway. Attempt is made on her life at two safe houses."

"What?" Nick read, "An attempt is made on Mrs. Thorne's life at the first safe house ten days after arrival." Nick skipped the location and read on. "An unknown person or persons stepped up to her bedroom window at two a.m., broke the window with the gun and fired a shot toward the bed. The witness was in the bathroom at the time. Searched for the perp but never apprehended."

"I'll be damned." Wonder how they knew where to find her? He turned to the next page. Second safe house twelve days later. "Man disguised as police officer. Walked into safe house claiming orders to change witness location. ID recognized as fake by guard. Attempted kidnapping failed." He skipped over the officer's name and rank. "Perp shot and killed by officer. Known Vargas man. Witness moved to third safe house.

"What the hell?" How did he get a uniform? How did they know where to find her? Questions kept twirling around inside his head. The one that bothered him the most—could there be a mole in the department? It had been seven days since the last attempt. He now understood why the captain chose him to protect her and why he wanted it done ASAP. He would succeed at this job or die trying.

****

A witness to murder?

Samantha Chadwick-Thorne?

How in the world had she ever gotten herself into such a mess? She sat on the uncomfortable bed, her face buried in her hands. Mother would have a massive coronary if she knew that her daughter, a Chadwick from one of the oldest families in upstate New York, was now living in a safe house under police protection.

Samantha uncovered her eyes to stare out the bedroom window. After what she had been through this past September, fall would never be her favorite time of the year again.

A hard knock on the door made her heart race. A wave of uneasiness flowed over her. Who could it be?

"Mrs. Thorne?"

Samantha stared at the door. "Who-who is it?" How she hated being afraid. It made her stutter and act like an abused dog. She rose from the bed.

"Detective Nick O'Reilly. Homicide. Kirkland Police Department."

"How do I know you are a real detective?"

She heard him mumble something to Dave, the policeman, guarding her door.

"It's okay. He's legit," the officer yelled. Relief flooded through her. Samantha's knees wobbled, and she grabbed onto the stuffed chair next to her. Right now, she couldn't be more grateful for Dave.

The door opened.

Detective O'Reilly stood well over six feet, making her crane her neck to look him in the eyes, which were covered with dark thin-rimmed mirrored glasses. A lock of his coffee colored hair rested on his forehead. His broad shoulders, twice the size of hers, stretched the seams of his black leather jacket and T-shirt. As tight and old as they were, he looked comfortable in his faded black jeans and well-worn boots. All he needed was a motorcycle and a helmet inscribed with the word, *Perfection*.

Definitely the type of man her mother had always ordered her to avoid. Mother could rest easy. She wasn't interested. Yet, he caused something to stir in her.

"Relax." Detective O'Reilly entered the room. "I'm your new babysitter."

6

The depth of his voice made butterflies flutter in her stomach, then, scatter in all directions. What did this man have to make her react this way? This had never happened to her before.

"Thank you just the same, Detective, but this nice gentleman is all I need." She smiled at the man standing behind Detective O'Reilly.

"My orders change things." O'Reilly's jaw muscles jumped.

"What, may I ask, would your orders be, Detective?"

"To keep you alive."

Samantha covered her mouth. Did he have to be so blunt?

O'Reilly turned to Dave, "I'll take it from here. You're to report to Captain Bianco."

"Will do."

Samantha overcame the shock of Detective O'Reilly's words in time to say, "Thank you, Officer Dave. You've been wonderful." She wanted to give him a hug for his many kindnesses to her, but she clung to the chair to keep her legs from folding beneath her.

He turned to leave. "It's been my pleasure. Be safe, Mrs. Thorne."

Without a word, Detective O'Reilly removed his glasses, then wandered around the room. He checked under and around the single bed and other skimpy furniture. He opened the closet door. Using both hands, he felt around the doorframe and the bar holding her clothes. He stepped back and closed the door. Then he stopped his hunt long enough to glance at her over his shoulder before continuing.

"What in the world are you searching for?"

His eyes were the color of a dark yummy chocolate bar. What was she thinking? She couldn't remember having such thoughts about her husband's eyes.

"Just checking."

The thoroughness of the man pleased her. Even this safe house warranted his scrutiny. Would he be the one to protect her from Chico Vargas? She shook away the thought. Trust no one. That's what life had taught her. She must not forget it.

"The room's clean. Sit." He motioned to the chair. "We need to talk." He tucked his glasses in his T-shirt pocket.

Did he think her a dog? She whipped around and moved toward the window.

"Suit yourself, but you make a great target over there."

Samantha hadn't thought about that and quickly stepped away from the window, never removing her gaze from Detective O'Reilly. He slouched down in the only stuffed chair in the room and drew out a weathered black notebook from his hip pocket. When he pulled the left side of his jacket open revealing his weapon, the horror of that night four weeks ago came rushing back. With a quick intake of breath, she stepped back against the wall.

A gun had killed her husband.

The same one almost killed her.

Fear overcame her every time she thought of the night Edward died. Her heart beat rapidly and perspiration broke out on her forehead. She gave herself a mental shake and willed herself not to fall apart in front of this man. The detective was a policeman. At least his gun should be friendly.

Or was it?

****

Nick took his time settling in the chair in hopes that Mrs. Chadwick-Thorne would plunk her well-shaped rear down, too. His captain pegged it correctly. She was a looker. The picture in her file should be tossed. Her strawberry blonde ringlets bounced and recoiled like little springs when she moved. She couldn't be more than five-two and her eyes were the most beautiful deep emerald green he'd ever seen. They'd been like a sucker punch in the gut the first time he looked into them.

Forget it man. You don't need to go down that road again.

Nick stood and offered her the soft chair. He opened his notebook and clicked his pen.

"Just have a seat." He pointed to the chair he vacated. Nick's style didn't include begging. He felt uncomfortable getting this woman to talk to him. Her jumping at every sound or sudden movement and the constant entwining of her hands bothered him. No woman should be this scared.

What I wouldn't give for a cigarette right now.

Instead, he pulled a miniature Tootsie Roll from his pocket and offered it to her. She shook her head. "Suit yourself." He took the paper off and popped the candy in his mouth. He chewed and waited for her to speak. After several minutes, she moved to the chair and sat on the edge.

She fidgeted with a button on her stark white blouse. Silk, no doubt, he thought. The navy pants she wore looked like they had been tailor-made by some fancy designer. Nick blocked the bad memories to concentrate on his notebook and give her a moment to relax.

"I've got a few questions."

Samantha straightened her back and looked him in the eyes. "I've told the whole thing over and over again to various police officials. Just read the reports I've already given."

That's my girl. Be strong. He'd rather have her sassing him than scared silly. He felt like a heel, but he needed to hear the details from her. That's the way he did things—the way he got a real feel for a case.

Nick shrugged his shoulder. "You didn't tell *me*, Mrs. Thorne," he replied in a quiet tone. "Neither of us has a choice. My boss made me your baby-sitter until you testify. My orders are to make sure you keep breathing." His gaze locked with hers. "And I always do my job," he finished in a tone that left no doubt.

Samantha leaned back against the chair but avoided his eyes. "This is my third safe house. Ha. Safe house. What a joke. That awful man's men tried to kill me in the first one, and to kidnap me from the second. Now you think you can protect me? What makes you think you'd succeed?"

Nick crossed his arms over his chest and stared at her. "Because...I know my job." He remained silent until she looked at him. "And I'm good at what I do."

"You're so confident, Detective O'Reilly."

"Yep, I am."

Those eyes. Jumping jacks in his mid-section told him he wasn't immune to her. Lust and key witness didn't belong in the same thought. Not on this job. Not in this lifetime. He leaned over, and then placed a hand on each arm of her chair and looked her in the eyes.

Giant error he knew, but he did it anyway.

"You'll be safe with me. That's a promise."

"I haven't been since—"

"You will be now," he said in a no-nonsense tone. He studied her a moment. The doubtful look in her eyes spoke louder than words. In her position, he wouldn't either. Two attempts on her life in official safe places would scare the pants off even the bravest witness. The fact that she was trembling in her expensive designer shoes didn't escape him. She covered it well. Her ritzy boarding school control training must be kicking in. Good! She'd need it.

Nick pushed away from her to grab a nearby wooden chair and straddled it. "What happened that night?"

After several tense moments of him staring at her very pale face, he was relieved when she took a deep breath and let it out. She stared at the wall and appeared to have put herself somewhere else. Maybe back in time to that night. He cursed himself for putting her through this again. He didn't abuse women. Why was he making her do this? Then she began to speak in a well-rehearsed monotone, what he knew to be her worst nightmare.

"I was awakened by loud voices about one o'clock in the morning." She stopped. Looked at Nick. Tears filled her eyes. Her hands trembled. "I'll n-never forget the t-terror I heard in Edward's voice. He was pleading for his life." A tear dropped down her cheek.

"Take it easy, Mrs. Thorne. I know this is hard on you." He gave her a tissue from the dresser. He reached in his pocket. "Want a drink? Candy?"

"No. I just want this whole thing to be over."

He wanted to tell her everything would be all right, but he knew otherwise. The next two weeks before the trial started weren't going to be easy for either of them.

"Give yourself a break. You've been through a hell of a trauma." She closed her eyes and turned away. He could see her struggle to keep her tears contained. What a bastard he was to make her live through this horror one more time. He felt her pain, and it ripped him apart. Emotions had no place in this job he reminded himself.

"Tell me about the man who shot at you."

Mrs. Thorne rubbed the side of her face with her open hand. "The foyer light was on. I don't know how he missed me the first time. For a brief moment, I found myself staring into the coldest, meanest eyes I had ever seen." Her body shook with a huge shiver. "I can't get the sight of those eyes out of my head."

"They'll fade with time," he hoped, trying to calm her. He doubted they ever would. "The report says you were injured?"

"Just a scratch." She rubbed a spot on her left shoulder. "It's a constant reminder of…"

Nick watched the memory ricochet through her mind. A bone-jarring shudder rocked her once again. She hugged herself. Nick started to remove his jacket.

She shook her head. "No. I'm okay."

"You sure there's nothing I can get you?"

"Thanks, but no." Still hugging herself, she continued, "He s-shot me. I s-screamed. Then both men hurried toward the stairs. That's when I realized they were coming after me. And I'd better get away or I would be…dead, too. I ran into my bedroom and locked the door."

"Smart move. It gave you the time you needed to

escape through the hidden stairway."

"Yes. I ran into the bathroom and grabbed a towel to wrap around my arm. I rushed into my walk-in closet seconds before the killers started pounding on my bedroom door. I heard a shot as I shut the door to the passageway. I always kept a flashlight there and used it to find my way to the underground root cellar at the back of our property. I called the police from a neighbor's house. You know the rest." With tears forming in her eyes, she stiffened her back. "Edward had no knowledge of the hidden stairway that led from his study. If he had, he might be alive today." Samantha looked away, biting her lip.

Nick would bet his Tootsie Rolls Edward's chances to escape were zero. He didn't want her to suffer any more than necessary, but he had a job to do. What she told him might save her life again someday. "So, this is your family home, which is why your husband had no knowledge of the passageways?"

She nodded. "They were my secret for years."

"Did your parents know about them?"

"They thought my grandfather had sealed all entrances years ago." Her lips curved in a slight smile. "Gramps took me on an *underground tour,* that's what he called it, on my eighth birthday. He told me fleeing slaves had passed through those hidden walls to their freedom years ago. He also added, 'We'll keep them a secret from your mom and pop cause you, my sweet child, might need to do a little escaping yourself someday.'"

"Your gramps was right." Nick made a note on his pad. "I've got to admire your courage. Not many society gals have your backbone."

"Thank you, I think." She was quiet for a moment. "I love my house, passageways and all."

"The house must be real old."

She nodded. "It was built around eighteen fifty."

Talking about her home made her face light up. Enchanting is the only word he could think of to describe her at that moment. He wished he could feel the same about his childhood home.

"That's quite a history."

"One of which I'm extremely proud." Samantha leaned forward. "May I please stand up now?"

"Sure."

Nick unfolded himself from the chair and stepped aside. Before he could help her, she stood and hurried toward the window. He stuck his notebook and pen in his inside jacket pocket, lifted the chair and set it back where he found it. He turned toward her and saw a flash outside the window.

He flew at her.

Chapter 2

Samantha's head crashed against the wall.

"Oomph." Stars exploded before her eyes. A wild thumping echoed in her ear, the one buried against a hard, muscular chest. Arms of steel wrapped her in a vise grip. She could feel every flex of his steely muscles, every heavy breath filling his lungs. A hint of citrus invaded her senses.

Detective O'Reilly had her pinned to the wall.

Samantha felt safe for the first time in weeks.

"You okay?" Nick whispered in her ear.

His warm breath against her face made those butterflies flutter again. "Just dazed a little." She shook her head in a desperate effort to tear her thoughts away from how this man made her feel. "Did I hear a gunshot or was that my skull cracking?"

"Right the first time."

A chill crawled up her spine. "No. N-Not again."

"You're safe now." He moved his head back away from her and studied her face. "You sure you're okay?"

"Yes, thanks to you."

"That's why I'm here," he growled. "I need to check things out. Don't move."

Samantha nodded. That she could do.

Detective O'Reilly stepped back, taking his warmth with him. Samantha wanted to yank him back, to feel secure in his arms once again. Not wanting to be a wimp, she managed a strong, "Be careful."

"Always." Nick moved the curtain, checking the outside before heading for the door. "Be right back. Stay put."

"Yes, sir." She had gotten the message the first time. The room began to spin and then darkened. Samantha leaned her head against the wall. She wrapped her arms around her waist and fought the blackness overpowering her. She raised her head. She stood, straight as she could. No way would she give into her fear. Fainting at this man's feet would be unacceptable. Undignified.

At the door, Nick stopped to look back at her. "Remember. You're mine for the next two weeks. I prefer you alive." He winked at her.

She rubbed the wiggling feeling in her stomach away with a shaking hand. She didn't *belong* to anyone, no less a *cop*. Someone rushed up the stairs.

"Everything okay, O'Reilly?" a woman asked.

"Just dandy. Did you see anyone?"

"They were gone by the time I got around to that side of the house. I did hear a vehicle move out at a high speed around the corner."

"I'll check it out." He waved a hand in Samantha's direction. "Meet Mrs. Chadwick-Thorne. This is Detective Amy Bauer. She'll take good care of you."

Samantha nodded and rubbed the back of her head.

Running down the stairs, O'Reilly yelled, "Keep her away from the window, Bauer."

"He thinks I'm an idiot. Guess I am, standing in front of a window like that," she mumbled.

"No. He's just cautious." Bauer smiled, moving farther into the room. "O'Reilly is also good at giving orders."

"I've noticed."

Being controlled all her life by her parents was one thing. Now, she had a bodyguard stepping up to take his turn. All she ever wanted in life was the freedom to make her own choices. She would be free to do just that after the trial and her life got back to normal.

A delayed reaction to the last few minutes set in. The brave façade she put on moments ago slipped away—fast. The shakes hit big time. She slid down the wall, sat and rested her head on her knees. She would control this attack of nerves, too.

Chico Vargas would not rule her life. How she wished she'd never heard of the man. He and his henchman occupied a suite in the county jail, where he still managed to carry out his evil ways. She wasn't so naive as to believe Vargas just wanted to scare her. If Nick hadn't been blessed with quick instincts...Samantha owed her life to a man she had known for less than an hour. A man she found herself angry with one minute and attracted to the next. She covered her face in her hands. "It's got to be the stress," she whispered to herself.

"You okay, Mrs. Thorne?"

"What? Oh, yes. Detective...ah..."

"Bauer, ma'am. If you need anything, let me know."

"Thank you." Samantha closed her eyes. At least she didn't order her away from the window. "I just wish this would all come to an end."

"You're going to be okay. Detective O'Reilly is a rebel, but he's the best." Detective Bauer smiled, but maintained her position at the door.

A nod was all Samantha could manage. The attractive brunette, dressed in plain black slacks and matching waist-length jacket, looked no more like a policewoman than she did. But at least someone, besides the man himself, believed in Detective O'Reilly's abilities. Her confidence in him went up a couple notches.

She'd learned one thing since her husband's untimely death—rely on no one. That included O'Reilly. She had one priority—staying alive to put Vargas behind bars permanently. Then no one would control her again.

She stared at the officer standing guard at the door. How could she stop these attempts on her life? Her mind reeled with possibilities.

Of course! Why hadn't she thought of it before? Vargas would do anything to get his greedy hands on a certain pouch. And she knew where to find it. She had one problem. How to get home to get it? Persuade Detective O'Reilly. A difficult job she knew, but she was up to the task.

Nick stomped up the stairs and into the room. "We're out of here."

"Did you find the gunman?"

"Nope." Nick hurried over to the bed, snatched up the pillow and stripped off the cover. He opened the small closet door wrapped his arms around the few clothes hanging there and pushed them in the pillowcase.

"What are you doing?"

"Packing." He proceeded to shove the pieces hanging over the edge into the case.

"Quit that. You'll ruin my things." She rushed over

and yanked a blouse out of his hands. He snatched the piece of silk away from her once again and packed it.

"Better a few pieces of cloth than you."

"I beg your pardon. They are more than cloth."

"No doubt." He opened the top drawer of the dresser and almost had his big hands on her lavender lacey bra.

She grabbed his wrist and eagle-eyed him. "Don't. You. Dare."

He glared back at her and then down at his arm. She got the message loud and clear. "Then don't touch my personal things," she ordered before releasing her hold on him.

A smile pulled at the corner of his lips. Detective Bauer chuckled from her place by the door.

How dare he handle her intimate clothing? Heat flooded her face. "Don't say it, Detective O'Reilly."

Nick pointed toward her bras and panties. "Pack those beauties or I will."

"Oh, for goodness sake. Give me that pillowcase." She yanked it from his hands and put the underwear in it as fast as she could. The less he saw of her personal things the better she would feel.

When she'd finished, he pulled the bag out of her hand, threw it over his left shoulder and took her arm with the other hand. "Let's go."

"Where are we going?" she said, tugging her arm free.

"Away." He grabbed her again.

When they reached the door, Detective Bauer was already on her way down the stairs. "Bauer?" She stopped and looked up. "Call the captain. Let him know what happened here. Then meet me at the airport."

"You don't want me to follow you?"

"No."

"You're the boss." Bauer turned and continued on her way.

Samantha tried to free herself from the grip he had on her arm. "Let me go. I learned to walk when I was ten months old."

His grip lessened, but he didn't release her, dragging her out into the hallway. "Glad to hear it. Now move those tootsies." Nick continued down the stairs. "Lady, you're lucky to be breathing. Let's keep you that way."

She had no argument with that.

He stopped at the outside entrance. "Now, be a good little girl. Do as you're told."

Her chin shot up, her back straight. "I'm not a little girl."

He eyed her from head to toe and back again. "Yep, you're right."

"You're no little boy either," she blurted out. The sudden rush of warmth to her neck and face brought back the heated memory of how she felt with him wrapped around her. "Oh, I didn't mean that the way…"

"Didn't you?" He raised his eyebrows.

"Are you always so…so blunt?"

"Yep."

****

Nick wanted to forget the close contact he'd felt with Samantha during the recent attempt on her life. It was tough to erase the feeling of all those soft curves glued to his body. Sure, he enjoyed the contact. What breathing male wouldn't? She smelled of intoxicating dreams and delicate woman. Her skin reminded him of an expensive Scotch—smooth and smoky. Running after the gunman saved him from making a damned fool of himself.

One thing for certain, that gunshot increased the urgency of his job. He needed her in a fighting mood.

"Come on. Admit it. You know you loved our little dance back there." He grinned. "All those little whimpers and snuggles."

"I do not whimper." Her chin shot up two inches. "And you, sir, are no gentleman."

"Aw. Now you've hurt my feelings." He gave her one of his brightest smiles. He noticed she did this upward push of her chin whenever she was in a huff. He had a feeling he'd be seeing a lot of it during the next two weeks.

"You're proud of your crude behavior, aren't you?"

"Good. You've learned I'm not one of your rich stuffed shirts." She glowered at him.

He nodded his head toward the door. "Let's travel."

Nick opened the back door to the house and checked for signs of the shooter. Satisfied things were safe, he pulled Samantha along behind him. Bauer, who had moved the car to within inches of the door and released the passenger seat back, waited, gun ready. He opened the car door and shoved Samantha into the front passenger seat.

"Down on the floor," he ordered. He tossed her belongings in the back. She didn't make a peep, but her steady glare spoke volumes. She sank to the floor on her knees, resting her arms and upper body on the seat.

"Thanks for the help, Bauer. See you at the airport."

"Any time." Bauer headed for her car.

Keeping a watchful eye, he slammed the door and hurried to get behind the wheel of the rusted Chevy. "We're off. Keep your head down."

"Don't you ever clean this vehicle?" She tossed a couple French fry boxes to the back along with several hamburger wrappers and empty bags. "It looks and smells like the local landfill." A couple of drink containers flew over the seat and bounced off the back window.

"This jalopy may not be one of your luxurious limousines, but it's all mine. Get used to it. You might have to survive worse things in the next two weeks."

Her head bobbed up from where she was crunched up on the floor. "Keep down. We don't know who's out there."

"Take me home," she demanded, lowering her head once again.

He chuckled.

"I'm serious."

"And I'm not?"

Samantha's huge sigh echoed in the car. "Listen. I really need to get some things before we continue on this journey."

Nick's lips drew tight across his teeth. His captain's plan didn't include taking her home.

"They wouldn't allow me back in my own house after the…"

Something inside him wanted to give in to her pleas. She pushed a strand of curly hair behind one delicate ear. The sudden flash of the rocks on her finger almost blinded him. That was something else he'd have to handle.

"Did you forget to pack your gifts of stolen baubles?" He saw anger cross her face before she lowered her head.

Why did her jewels make him so angry? He could care less about them. A voice in the back of his head kept screaming that he was jealous because he came from a dirt-poor family.

Jealous! Hell. No. There's no way he could afford expensive jewels for any woman on a cop's salary. That had been proven to him by an expert.

"I don't want anything he gave me."

Nick's gaze snapped to hers where he saw the truth reflected in dark green pools. "Good. We're heading to the airport."

"We can enter the house through the secret passageway, and no one will know we've been there." Samantha placed her hand on his leg. She yanked it back. Her hand hit the dash. A loud crack of fragile knuckles filled the car. "Darn."

"You okay?"

"Fine!"

The instant she touched him, a red-hot electrical shock slammed into his groin. By the way she jerked back her hand, he knew she felt it too.

"The police have the place under surveillance. Vargas must have his watchdogs out, too. You got away from them before. They won't take a chance of it happening again."

She touched his leg again. "I'm not in the habit of begging, but…"

He stared at her hand then at her. "Is that an

invitation, Mrs. Thorne?"

"What? Oh." She pulled her hand away once again. "No. Uh…I—"

Nick arched his brow. "Where I come from, it is."

Her chin shot up. "It's obvious we don't come from the same place."

She's indignant again. He chuckled to himself. She had that one right. They came from miles apart on the social track. Nick knew he'd regret asking the next question but did it anyway. "What's so important in the mansion that you'd risk your life to get?"

"I want different clothes. I've been wearing these for a month." She motioned to her white blouse and navy pants. "I'd like to get some makeup and…ah…woman things. I need to feel like a human being again."

"You got any more of those fancy bras at home?" She gave him one of those "you-are-so-crude" glares. He snickered. He understood her need to be normal. He'd had a few of those times himself. She'd put in a hellish month. It's a wonder she still had it together.

Taking her home went against all the rules of the academy and many more he'd learned the hard way. But when had he ever gone by the book? Doing what he thought best kept him alive. He made the mistake of peeking at her out of the corner of his eye. The sad pleading expression on her face tore at his heart, causing him to change course and make his way to money row.

Nick glanced at his watch. Their flight left in two hours. They'd just about have time. "Hang on. We've got a tail to lose."

"Thank you."

"Don't thank me yet." He stepped on the gas and made a sharp right turn, then a left, another left and then a right into a parking garage and stopped. He hated the way she was bouncing around like a rubber ball being thrown against the wall, but he had no choice if he wanted to lose this tail following them. A black sedan went speeding by the entrance. Nick made a quick U-turn and headed in the opposite direction.

"Tell me again where this secret entrance is located."

****

Fifteen minutes later, Samantha lifted the latch on the stairway door that led into the walk-in closet. She gave a mental sigh of relief. Once again, she thanked her ancestors for their foresight. As a child, she had considered sneaking out without being detected a great adventure. During her teen years, the passageway proved to be a convenient way to meet the friends who didn't make her mother's approved list, Edward being one of them. She'd used it to escape the hell her marriage had become once she discovered Edward was fencing jewels. A month ago, that same secret hallway saved her life.

Nick swore.

She glanced back, swinging the flashlight in his direction. "Is something wrong?" She couldn't help but snicker to herself every time he grumbled. He kept hitting his head on the large stones in the wall and had problems squeezing through smaller sections of a cave-like structure.

"Why didn't you tell me this place was made for leprechauns?" He rubbed his head. "Hard stone is rough on a man."

"Not many men were your size in the eighteen hundreds." If looks were rockets, she'd be landing on Mars about now. She chuckled. "You have cobwebs in your hair."

"And that's funny how?"

The warmth of his nearness made her tingle all over, erasing any comeback that she might have made. Samantha opened the passageway door leading into her closet. Her lungs filled with the humid stale air, making her cough.

All her beautiful things had been ripped off their hangers and thrown to the floor. She stepped over the mound of her belongings and through the closet doorway into her bedroom.

"Oh, my goodness." This is what Vargas and his henchman had done while she was fleeing for her life.

Her favorite bedside lamps were smashed. The dressers stripped inside and out; the mattress lay in shreds.

Nick gave a long, loud whistle. "I wonder if they found what they were looking for."

She watched him take in everything in the room. He didn't appear to miss a thing. Did he know more than he was saying? "What do you mean?"

"This kind of mess? They were looking for something." He turned to her. "Did they find it?"

Samantha was stunned. Her insides quivered, and she felt sick to her stomach. She picked up what was left of her favorite Monet painting and leaned the tattered canvas against the wall. After pulling the bedspread up on part of the bed, she sat down. "I feel very violated."

"No doubt, but you didn't answer my question."

"I didn't stop to ask their reasons for killing my husband and whether or not they found what they came here to get. I was running for my life." What would he do if he knew how close to the truth he had come?

"We've got a plane to catch. Let's move it. This place gives me the creeps."

"My large suitcase is down in the basement." Getting him to the other end of the house for a few minutes was a necessity. "It's the only door on the right in the kitchen."

"We don't have time for that. Use a pillowcase or a sheet." He stepped toward the bathroom. "Are they in here?"

"No, Detective O'Reilly. I will not put my good clothing in a pillowcase, or a sheet, again." Samantha stood at the doorway to the stairs and pointed. "That way!"

Nick stared at her, his eyes slits. She held her head high and tried to look as confident as she could.

"Make it fast. Being here is dangerous." Nick swaggered out of the room whistling, letting her know he gave the orders.

She listened for Nick's steps on the balcony, then on the steps and the foyer below before inhaling. She hadn't dared to breathe for fear he would refuse to do as she ordered. She rushed back to the closet and into the hidden stairwell.

She located and removed the loose rock, retrieving the small leather bag she had put there six weeks ago, the same night Edward had given it to her promising her to never reset another stolen jewel. A promise he managed to break within hours of making it. She pushed the rock back into place and returned to the bedroom.

A door opened downstairs.

Samantha ran into the bathroom and grabbed a jar of her face cream still intact on the vanity. She opened the pouch. A precious jewel-studded gold antique cross glittered back at her. It had a large one-karat perfect diamond in the center with four half-karat red rubies on each of the four tips. Several small sapphires covered the rest of it. Samantha had never seen anything so spectacular. She could understand why Vargas wanted it back.

Her hands were shaking in her haste to get the lid off the jar and tuck the two-inch work of art inside under the cream. She washed and dried her hands. She took a deep breath and exhaled. Another task finished. She hurried back to the bedroom to find a sheet of her personalized writing paper and a pen. Then she wrote:

If there are any further attempts on my life, you'll never see the cross again.

She folded the letter, jammed it into an envelope, addressed it to Vargas at the county jail and shoved it in her purse. She hurried to the safe that was no longer hidden behind a portrait. It didn't appear to have been touched. Most of the Chadwick jewels were in a safe-deposit box in the bank, but her two favorite pieces were locked in here. The dial shot past the first number. "Darn."

Would she ever stop being nervous? She got the safe open on the second try and removed the jewelry box along with a roll of large bills. She rammed the bills in her tote styled bag, knowing she would need them in the days ahead. She set the box on the dresser and opened it. The gems danced in the sunlight streaming through the window. Samantha selected the felt purse containing her great-grandmother's ruby necklace and diamond brooch and dropped them in her bag, too. The rest…well, she wanted no part of stolen jewels. She closed the lid.

"The cross!"

The jar was still on the vanity. She heard Nick on the stairs saying something about the bullet holes in the wall. She rushed to the bathroom. If Nick found out about the cross, he'd make her turn it in to the police. Or worse yet, accuse her of being Vargas' accomplice. Without it, she'd have no bargaining tool.

He entered the bedroom as she came out of the bathroom with two jars in hand.

"Here, let me." Nick reached for them with his free hand.

She turned sharply to avoid his grasp. "No thanks, I can manage." The jar with the cross slipped out of her hand and fell to the floor. Samantha closed her eyes, afraid to look.

"Lucky on that one, Mrs. Thorne." He retrieved the jar and read the label. "Ginseng Facial Moisturizer."

Only then did Samantha dare to open her eyes. "Give that to me before you break it," she managed to croak. Before she could get her hands on it, he tossed it in the air. She watched it fly and land in his large hand. Her heart stopped, then raced. She snatched it from him. "Stop that," she yelled and hurried to put the jars in her bag.

Nick set the luggage on the dresser and opened it for her. "Hustle, will ya?" He walked over to the curtain and peeked out. "Hmmmmm. What's he doing here?" he mumbled.

"Who?"

"My partner."

"Detective Bauer? I thought she was on her way to the airport."

"She is. Mike is my partner."

"Isn't this his case?" Samantha folded a blouse and set it in the case.

"No." He glanced back at her. "I don't like this. We need to get moving."

"Be ready shortly." She placed each piece of clothing in the case taking care to press out any creases.

"Why are you here, Mike?" Nick mumbled to himself. He glanced back at her. "Hey. We don't have all day. Throw those rags in there."

"I beg your pardon. They aren't rags. They're—"

"Custom made, I know. We don't have time to worry about wrinkles. Throw 'em in or I will." He turned back to the window.

Samantha wanted to sit down and refuse to move. She was tired of being ordered around.

Nick turned to face her. The look he gave her brooked no argument. She hated him right now, but she began to toss her clothing into the case. After all, he'd done her a favor bringing her home. When she finished packing, she picked up the jewel case.

"What's that?" Nick nodded toward the box.

She stared at him debating whether to tell him the truth. What did it matter? The police would want the jewels anyway. "The jewelry Edward gave me."

"All those sparkles didn't make you happy?"

"At the time, I was ecstatic." That was an eternity ago.

"Let's see." Nick walked toward her.

She unlatched the lid and flipped it open. Little sparkles of light flickered on Nick's well-tanned face. He blew a long slow whistle.

"That much loot is hard to give up."

"I don't want them." At his surprised look, she added, "How many of them do you think came from stolen jewelry?"

"Hard to say. Maybe none."

"Or all of them. Edward claimed all his gifts were legal gems, but I didn't believe him. I stopped believing him months ago." Samantha pushed the box at Nick. She grinned when he fumbled to catch it. "And I don't want these." She tugged at her wedding rings and threw them in the box. In seconds, she closed the lid, yanked it out of his hands and placed the box back in the safe.

Nick wondered about the relationship between Samantha and Edward. Not much love or trust between the two of them. How could she not know what was going on?

Or was she an accomplice?

Those wedding rings alone must be worth a few grand. She had tossed them around like cheap junk from a dollar store. Either she should be given an Oscar for her winning performance or the lady was being bluntly honest. His gut told him the latter was the truth, but he couldn't rule out the former. He would protect her but with wide-open eyes.

Nick wandered over to the window once again. His mind swirled with questions he'd get the answers to soon. He could still see Mike leaning against the car and chatting with the stakeout team. Something wasn't right here. The Thorne murder wasn't Mike's case. Mike laughed, pushed away from the car and crossed

the street, on a direct path to Samantha's house.
What was he doing here?
And alone?

Chapter 3

"Fool!" Chico Vargas yelled.

"But…" Alonzo stammered.

"Do not but me," Chico growled in his native Spanish. "To kill her, no. To bring her to me, yes." He brought his fist down hard on the table and cursed.

The officer guarding the visitor's room in the county jail stepped toward Vargas. "Control yourself, or you're done here," he ordered.

Vargas waved him back. "Okay. Okay." He knew he'd be out of there pronto or a few politicians would wish for death. The guard took his position by the door and crossed his arms over his chest.

Vargas pointed a finger at Alonzo and lowered his voice. "Your brains are missing, huh?"

"She lives. If I shoot to kill, she'd be dead."

Vargas waved his comment away. "Yet, she got away. Yes?"

"I've got one of the guys on her. She won't get far."

"Better for you if you bring her here. We are short on time. *Santo Maria. W*ay short. He closed his eyes against the thought the death of his family if he didn't find the cross in the next ten days.

****

Back in the car and on the road again, Samantha asked, "Where are we going?"

"Airport." Nick checked the rearview mirror before glancing her way. When she was in a snit, her cheeks flushed and fire danced in her big beautiful eyes. For some perverse reason, he liked getting a reaction from her.

"Would it be asking too much to inquire what city?"

"Yep." He looked back at the road.

"You're a frustrating man." Samantha crossed her arms over her chest and stared out the front window.

"Yeah?"

"Darn—"

"Tut-tut." Nick scolded her, wiggling his index finger back and forth in her direction.

Nick made a sharp turn into an interstate rest area and stopped the car.

"What are you doing? Is someone following us?" Samantha turned to look behind them.

"Maybe."

"Isn't this dangerous? We're just asking to be caught, sitting here waiting."

"I've got something for you." He pulled a small box from his pocket. He couldn't believe he was doing this. He'd made a vow no gal would ever wear his ring again. The one time he attempted marriage had been an embarrassing big flop.

"Here." He tossed the box at her. It bounced off the corner of her pocketbook. She grabbed and caught the box before it hit the floor. "Open."

She lifted the lid. Samantha's sudden intake of breath echoed in the silent car. "What's this?"

"Put it on." Nick's throat constricted, his voice cracked. Proposing marriage of any kind made him sick to his stomach.

"Never." She closed the box and tossed it back at him.

"Be realistic. We won't be married. We'll only be pretending. Have you ever done any acting?"

"Only all of my life. But this—"

"Then a couple more weeks won't matter. We'll be living together for the next two weeks. It'll be easier to refer to you as my wife." Had he really used those words—*my wife*? He never thought he'd say those two words together again.

"Why can't we just live together? Lots of couples do that today." The expression on her face brightened. "I know. I could be your sister."

"And share my room?"

First her jaw dropped. Then both eyebrows shot up. The brightness surrounding her disappeared. She looked so shocked, he laughed.

"I will not sleep with you." Samantha stiffened.

He bristled at her attitude. "Did I ask you to?" Was he that low on her social scale? He bet he rated next to worms and snakes. Did she think every man wanted to slip between her legs? Though that might be quite an experience for them both, it would never happen. He was on the job. He would protect her with his life. "Marriage is a convenience."

"Whose? Yours? Certainly, not mine."

"Just wear the damn ring." He took the gold band from the box and held her left hand. He shoved the ring on her finger. Samantha yanked her hand back.

Nick's patience came to an end. He got in her face and inhaled. Big mistake. His head spun from her sweet flowered scent. He wanted to leap from the car and hightail himself to the next state but held his ground. "We *will* share a room. I can't protect you with a wall between us."

The sound of her teeth grinding together echoed in his ear. Nick stared into the depths of her eyes, which anger had darkened to a deep green. "And you will sleep alone, Mrs. Thorne." A grin twitched at the corner of his mouth. He hesitated, lowered his voice, leaned closer and added, "Unless, of course, you beg me to—"

"Don't hold your breath, Detective."

Samantha turned and stared straight ahead, but not before Nick caught a subtle change in her expression. Was that amusement? Nick couldn't help smiling. It'd been a long time since he'd known a woman who could spar with him in a good verbal battle. What a time to find one. Yeah, he just might enjoy the next two weeks.

Nick leaned back in his seat and drove back on the interstate, willing himself to think like a cop. One thought kept bothering him. Was she as innocent in this mess as she wanted him to believe? Or was she the actress?

How could a woman not know her husband fenced stolen jewels? Didn't married couples confide in each other? Spill secrets? Didn't she ever visit Thorne's store? Check out the back room? Such questions twirled around in his head like a child's top on fast spin. He'd know the answers. Until then, he'd be on his guard keeping an eye out for her killers and/or accomplices.

"If we're going to make this inconvenient marriage work, shouldn't we be on a first name basis?" Samantha hugged her purse to her chest.

"Sure. Do you prefer Sam or Samantha?"

She thought for a minute. "I've never been called

Sam. My mother insisted everyone call me Samantha."

"What do *you* prefer?" He could care less what mama thought. Mama had already done too much controlling. Samantha's answer surprised him.

"I think I like…Sam."

"Then Sam it is. I'm Nick." She smiled. He admired her courage to change her life. Why not start with her name?

Calling her Sam would help him to think of her as just another guy. Who was he trying to fool? No way could he ever think of this beauty as a man. Not in this lifetime. He looked to the heavens and mumbled, "You were right, Ma. Explosives do come packaged in beautiful wrappings."

"Did you say something?"

"Naw." He shrugged his shoulders. "Talking to myself." He often had conversations with his mother, but only when he was alone.

They approached the air terminal. "Where are we going?"

"Airport." She sighed. Nick grinned to himself.

"What *city*? New York? Rochester?"

"Dallas."

"Texas?" she screeched in a high voice.

"Can you lower the volume? You're hurtin' my ears." Nick made a point of wiggling his index finger in his right ear.

"Why Dallas of all places?" Samantha lowered her voice and stared at him, her confusion obvious.

He shrugged his shoulders. "Why not?"

Moments later, they pulled into the parking garage and found a spot near the front. His partner, Mike, was scheduled to pick his car up later. Nick still couldn't figure out why Mike would be at Samantha's house. He didn't have time to sort out Mike's strange behavior right now, but he would.

Nick did a quick surveillance of the area. Satisfied, he said, "Stay put for a minute." He got out, walked around. His well-trained gaze took in the roof, then the parking lot. Two ladies, each toting a large suitcase and a small carry-on hurried toward the entrance where Detective Bauer stood. Two cars were pulling onto the off ramp. Bauer signaled the all clear. Nick got their luggage and opened her door.

"So far, so good." Nick helped her from the car. "Ready?"

"As I'll ever be, I guess."

"Walk in front of me and hurry. I'll be close behind."

She followed his orders. Nick's admiration for this witness climbed another notch. The view from her backside sure was a gorgeous eyeful, with perfect hips swaying with every step. He'd walk behind her anytime.

They approached the entrance door. Detective Bauer stepped in front of Samantha. She gasped and took a step back, knocking her suitcase out of Nick's hand. He grabbed the handle and nudged her forward with the luggage.

"Detective Bauer, ma'am, from the safe house?" She led the way to the correct terminal at a fast pace.

"Oh, yes, now I remember."

"Didn't mean to frighten you," Bauer said over her shoulder.

"I'm a little on edge these days. Is it safe here?"

"Yes, ma'am."

"Bauer's my backup until we leave." He could see the relief on Samantha's face. "Spot anything suspicious?"

"Negative."

"Maybe lady luck is smiling on us."

They checked their bags, went through security, and got on the plane without incident. Nick sat very attentive, checking out each person who entered and took a seat. The back of his neck prickled.

They were being watched.

Which passenger belonged to Vargas?

****

An hour into the flight and somewhere over the States, Samantha closed her magazine. Worrying over what the future would bring made concentrating impossible. She leaned her head back against the headrest and tried to take a nap. It proved to be impossible.

She stared at the ring Nick had insisted she wear. It felt like a gold bar straight from the vaults of Fort Knox. It couldn't have weighed more. She turned the ring with her thumb, thinking of Edward's proposal. Candlelight, music, flowers, the right words and a huge diamond had them traveling to Vegas and eloping the same night. Nick's proposal, such as it was, didn't compare. Of course, they weren't really married.

Samantha had known Edward only a few weeks before they married, but she knew less about Nick other than he had saved her life. But something about him made her ignorant hormones jump to full alert whenever he so much as glanced at her. Once again, she blamed her reaction on tension. It certainly wasn't the man. He was too arrogant and bossy to suit her.

"Missing your baubles already?"

Samantha jumped in her seat. She thought Nick would sleep the whole trip. "You must have a low opinion of me."

He shrugged his shoulder, straightened in his seat. "Got no opinions. Just observations."

"And what is your observation, Detective?" Now why was he frowning at her?

"Callin' me by your pet name in public sets my old heart a pumpin'," he whispered.

Pet name? Had the high altitude affected the man's brain? Before she could think of a comeback, he leaned over and nuzzled his face in her neck.

"Little passengers have giant ears," he whispered.

"Oh." He was right. Anyone could be a person sent to murder her. "I didn't think—"

"Be more careful." He raised his head and cupped her face with his large hand. "Let's try that again."

Stunned for a moment, she couldn't move. How would his strong arms feel wrapped around her while his lips tasted hers? His would taste like chocolate, she knew. Hers? Bad breath. Eating hadn't been a priority since she met the man. Would it matter to him? A coughing jag by someone in the back jarred her back to reality.

"Stop that." She leaned away from him.

He chuckled. "Is that any way to speak to your husband when he's giving you a little lovin'?"

Samantha forgot they were supposed to be married. "Sit back…huh…Nick."

"There you go." He slid his finger down her jaw and leaned back in his seat, smiling.

Her heart turned over in response. The touch of his

lips on her neck lingered. Oh, dear. She had been without affection for too long. Dating again would be her first priority after the trial. Yes. That's what she would do. The plane landed in Dallas and came to a stop at the gate. Nick surprised her by jumping up and grabbing her wrist. She just had time to seize her purse before he dragged her down the aisle.

"Miss? Miss? Quick, my wife is sick. The little darlin's pregnant you know," he whispered to the flight attendant loud enough for those near to hear. He wrapped his arm around Samantha's waist. "Lean on me, sweetheart. Try not to up chuck here." Then, "Hurry! I need to get her to a restroom."

The flight attendant pointed to the restroom door.

"She needs fresh air."

Samantha wondered what craziness Nick had gotten her into now, but knew he expected her to play her role. She grabbed her mouth. "I—"

"Don't talk, darlin', I wouldn't want you to spray these nice people. Miss?"

Passengers pulled away murmuring words like, "Let them out." "How disgusting." "Hurry up." "Poor thing." "Oh. Dear."

The flight attendant fumbled with the latch. At last, she opened the door. "This way, sir. The way is clear."

Thank goodness. The next thing she knew she was being hurried up the jet way to the main concourse with Nick whispering instructions in her ear.

"Now when you get—"

"The least you could've done is warn me. I've never been this embarrassed—"

"There's no time. In the restroom look for a lady wearing a white felt Stetson. Her name is Lucy. She will fill you in."

"A white hat? But—"

"No time for chit-chat. Look for Lucy." He raised his head and started yelling orders. "Please let us through. My wife is sick. You know how pregnant women are. This one is about to toss the peanuts and orange juice she had on the plane."

It worked again. His loud voice carried and cleared a path to the nearest restroom. It also gained them more attention than she wanted or thought wise under the circumstances.

Nick eased her through the doorway to the restroom. "Now go do your thing, darlin'. Make way ladies."

His loud ravings had put her at the head of a long line. That's exactly what he'd intended. A woman dressed in skin-tight jeans, a short faded, jean jacket, well-worn cowboy boots and sporting a white felt Stetson appeared at her elbow.

"Ya'll need some help, little mother-to-be."

Before she had time to react, she found herself pushed in the handicapped cubicle.

"I'm Lucy." Lucy put her fingers to Samantha's lips and pointed her thumb to the stall next to them. Then she motioned for her to kneel down and start gagging.

She got the message and played her part.

"Ya'll be right as rain on a Texas prairie in a minute, sweetie. Those little critters can make a mama awful sick at times." Lucy yanked off her long black wig and motioned for Samantha to put it on her head.

She looked first at the wig and then at Lucy. She sent a questioning look Lucy's way only to discover that she was peeling off her clothes and motioning for her to do the same. Had she lost her mind? She wasn't stripping in front of this woman.

"Nick tell you we were going to exchange?" she mouthed, motioning back and forth between them with her index finger.

Samantha shook her head no.

"That's Nick," Lucy mumbled under her breath and whispered, "This is part of the ruse. We're exchanging places and so is Nick with my partner."

"You want me to wear your clothes?" She couldn't. She wouldn't.

"You've got it."

"I only wear my own clothes." Samantha stood up. For goodness sakes. She had *never* worn hand-me-downs. In fact, others had worn her discarded clothing and been thrilled to get them. *Oh. My. Now I sound like my mother.*

"You will now." Lucy studied her for a second. "It's your choice. Exchange or be killed."

Samantha began unbuttoning her blouse. She'd do whatever it took to stay alive. Lucy handed her the backpack after completely exchanging their outer look. Samantha turned away from her to switch the contents of her designer purse to the cheap backpack. Though Lucy appeared to be clean, wearing someone else's clothing made her feel in need of a bath. She couldn't worry about that right now.

"Let's see how good you are at acting," Lucy whispered, opening the stall door and hustling her from the bathroom.

Samantha, in shocking silence, accepted gratitude from a "pregnant" Lucy now dressed in her custom-made clothes. Lucy's "worried husband" wore the clothes Nick had worn when she last saw him. This comedy act had better work, or they went to a lot of trouble for nothing.

A cowboy grabbed her hand. She didn't recognize him until he smiled. Nick looked like he'd just stepped off the range. He wore a faded, blue western styled work shirt and jeans, dust covered cowboy boots and a black Stetson. She spotted his blonde ponytail and fought back a giggle. He even wore a red and black neckerchief and sure looked like a cowboy.

"Come on, filly, we got a horse to ride." Nick grabbed her by the elbow and hustled her toward the exit.

"We what?" Samantha was sure she had misunderstood.

"You can ride, can't you?"

"Of course. But wouldn't a car be faster and safer?"

"Yep." Nick pulled her along until they were finally in the parking lot.

"What about our luggage?"

"It's going to Chicago."

"Chicago? But I thought…" She was glad she had the foresight to put the jewels, the letter, and the cross in her purse instead of the suitcase. Her luggage and her beautiful things were lost forever. "But they were—"

"Custom made. So you've said."

"What will I wear? I will not remain in these." Samantha pointed to Lucy's clothes."

Nick studied her new outfit. "Sexy. Real Sexy."

"Would you behave?"

"Impossible."

"That, I believe." She'd staple her mouth shut before admitting how warm his words made her feel. It'd been a long time since anyone had used such a word to describe her. It felt good!

The wonderful feelings she just experienced were soon erased by the way he continued to push her out of the door and into the parking area "Will you stop hurrying me? I'm tired of you manhandling me," she whispered.

"You know you love my hands on you."

"Ooooh." Under her breath she added, "And you, *sweetheart*, need lessons on how to be a gentleman."

Nick leaned close. "Now, *honey bun*, we've already settled that one."

She'd had enough and was about to refuse to move another inch when he stopped beside a large new black pickup with one of those shiny silver boxes in the back.

"I thought you said we were riding horses."

"Check under the hood." Nick pointed to the front end of the truck. "Several of them in there. We're in Texas. Everyone rides this kind of *horse* here."

"I thought you meant a real one. One with four legs."

"It's still a possibility." He wiggled his eyebrows.

"Have you ever ridden a horse?"

"Me? Huh…" Nick pulled on his earlobe.

"You haven't, have you?" The sheepish, little boy look he gave her made something flutter in her chest. She didn't understand her reaction. She brushed it away by giving him a satisfied smile and saying, "But I have. Many times."

"Well, hop on this one and let's ride."

Samantha fought the urge to salute him. Instead,

she crawled in the truck, clutching the backpack to her chest. He'd rushed her so she hadn't had a chance to mail the letter to Vargas. When they stopped for lunch, she'd find a way to put the letter in a mailbox. Satisfied with her plan, she settled back to enjoy the ride, praying that they had gotten away without being seen.

Chapter 4

Nick noticed a possible tail following them out of the airport. Several miles down the interstate it was still there. He took the ramp to the next exit. The car followed. Maybe their one-act play hadn't worked after all.

"Is someone following us?" Samantha turned to look out the back window.

"Maybe."

"Is it the red SUV or the dark blue truck?"

"The dark blue monster."

"Oh." She turned to face the road, tightening her arms around the denim backpack she held close to her chest.

He hadn't missed the trembling hands or the fact she clung to the pack like she would lose her life without it. Why? He didn't have time to find out now, but he would.

They stopped for a red light. "How are you at playing hide 'n seek?"

"Not very good, I'm afraid."

Nick turned to stare at her.

Samantha shrugged. "I always got caught."

"Watch and learn from an expert." He tromped on the gas and made a quick right turn a moment before the light turned. They rounded a curve and were out of sight in seconds. Then he made a sharp left-hand turn onto a gravel road and another abrupt turn, putting them behind a large clump of trees. He cut the engine, opened the windows, and listened. A few scared birds flew out of the trees. Then a quiet silence filled the air.

"I guess we lost them." He opened the door and slid out.

She crawled out and straightened her jean jacket. "We didn't fool them, then?"

He shrugged. "Maybe a false alarm. You okay?"

"I'm a little…" Her words faded as she twisted away.

Damn. He'd frightened her. Nick grabbed her by the shoulders and turned her to face him. He raised her chin with his index finger, forcing her to look at him. She closed her eyes.

"Don't be afraid. I'll protect you."

"It's not that. Well, yes, that too, but I…"

"Tell me?"

"You'll think me a little crazy."

"Maybe." He dropped his hands and rammed them in his pockets.

"I thought it was…exhilarating." She opened her eyes.

They sparkled. Her smile—radiant. She was beautiful. His heart forgot a beat. It took a moment before his brain and mouth could function together.

"You liked being chased by possible killers?" He said, not quite believing his ears.

"No. It was frightening, yet…exciting." She looked away briefly, before adding, "What can I say. I've lived a rather sheltered life."

"Sheltered and dull."

"Exactly. That's why this was…thrilling."

She touched something deep inside him. And he didn't like it. Or want it.

"I don't want to die," Samantha continued, "but that doesn't make a chase any less stimulating."

He rolled his eyes and shook his head. "Of course, it doesn't."

"Will we be hiding long? We missed lunch and I'm starving." She touched her hand to her stomach.

"Public places are too dangerous right now."

"Oh." Just then her stomach spoke its mind. Samantha pointed to her midsection. "She doesn't know that."

He grinned and jumped on the back of the truck. "Two lunches coming up." He unlocked and opened the silver carpenter box setting there. "Right on!" He tossed her an emergency survival blanket. "Set this out, will ya?" She caught it and hurried to lay it on the ground under the shade of a large tree. He carried the cooler to the blanket, lifted the lid.

"Ah, look what we have here." He waved two huge bags of Tootsie Rolls in the air. "Lucy knows better than to forget these." One of the bags he tossed on the blanket. The other he returned to the cooler.

They ate ham sandwiches and apples in silence. A car roared by now and then. None came down their road. Nick leaned against a tree where he could watch the road and Samantha. She sat on the blanket with her legs folded back beside her. He watched her delicate nibbles on the sandwich. Graceful and dignified like a princess.

Wearing hand-me-down clothes didn't change the "old money" look she wore about her like a pair of well-worn gloves. She appeared to be completely relaxed for the moment. Damn, this woman could be snobby as hell at times.

"So, you're not good at hide 'n' seek." Nick knew better than to check out her personal life, but somehow the words popped out of his big mouth.

"Terrible. I was always the first one caught."

He took a long swig of water. "Does that mean you didn't play basketball or volleyball either?"

"Goodness no."

"Didn't you want to?"

"Oh, I tried." A grin tugged at the corner of her mouth. "Due to my lack of talent, the coaches invited me to quit."

He laughed. "That bad, huh?"

"I'm not even good at being a wife."

"Who fed you that line?" Why would she say such a thing?

"I failed Wife 101. At least Edward thought so."

Nick was more inclined to believe Edward was a worthless piece of crap as a husband. Weren't debutantes trained to be good wives? Weren't heirs to fortunes married off to more money? The reminder of her wealth stopped him short. It brought back bad memories he never wanted to forget.

"So how did it feel to grow up a rich kid?" He mentally cursed himself. "Forget I mentioned it." He couldn't let his past get in the way of his job. Man, he was in for a long two weeks.

She studied him for a moment before responding. "What do you have against the affluent people?"

"Not a thing."

"It's apparent that you do."

Yeah, he did. Damn. He wished she'd stop looking

at him as though she could read every thought in his hard head.

Samantha looked him directly in the eye. "You'll tell me—eventually."

Her answer, so abrupt and certain, left him choking on a wise retort.

She turned her back to him. "My childhood and the way I was raised is no concern of yours."

"Just making conversation." The snobbish rich gal had returned.

She turned to face him. "Then let's talk about when you were a little boy."

"Let's not."

"Why? I think it's a great topic to discuss."

"I don't." He didn't want to remember his father's desertion, or how his old man had conned retired people out of their life savings. What a family heritage. Not something to brag about for sure.

"Then let's mutually agree not to discuss our childhoods."

"Sounds good to me." He guzzled his water; fascinated by the way she finished eating and then tapped her mouth with the napkin. No big swipes like he'd done. Another way they were different. She was the lady, he the tramp.

"It's beautiful here. Peaceful." Samantha crossed her legs Indian style and studied the countryside.

"Mmmm." He leaned his head back and closed his eyes.

"I often wonder what my life would have been like if I hadn't married Edward."

Uh, oh. What brought this on?

"How different would my life be today if I'd

married my family's choice?"

"You'd be with a *live* husband right now."

"Yes. But I wouldn't have loved him either."

He opened one eye to look at her. Interesting comment, he thought.

"Neither man loved me."

"Then why in hell did you marry Thorne?" That question jump-started Nick's mind. He opened the other eye. Is this her motive for Thorne's murder? She didn't love him, but hung around until she could find a way to get rid of him? Inherit his business? Remarkable what some people do for money.

"We each had our reasons for getting married. Besides, we did like each other."

"Like? As in friends?"

"Yes." She smiled. "I married him because my parents hated him. The fires of Hell raged hot in the Chadwick house for months after we eloped. Of course, they disliked him on sight. He didn't "socialize" with their circle of friends and his crude language annoyed them."

"He married you to tick off your parents?"

"Of course not. Though he did enjoy "ticking" them off. He married me for one thing—my money."

"You knew this?"

"Of course. We had a long conversation about it before we married."

"Great reasons to get hitched." Money sure hadn't been the reason his ex-fiancée had agreed to marry him.

"We thought so at the time." She picked a blade of grass and played with it.

"I feel a 'but' coming?"

"Revenge lasts such a short time. Then reality sets

in."

Her sadness made him want to give her a big hug, but he remained against his tree. "Meaning?"

"Don't you think we should leave?" Samantha got to her knees and started placing things back in the cooler. She picked up the bag of Tootsie Rolls.

He reached over and took them from her. In other words, butt out! "Hey, you started this conversation."

"And I'm ending it."

Nick studied her. Did he want to dig deeper for the truth? His doubts about her were screaming at him, but he dreaded to have them confirmed. Suppose she hired Vargas to kill her husband. Getting shot could be a ploy to confuse the police. What about the attempts on her life? Could it be a big conspiracy to make her look innocent? She hadn't been harmed after the initial injury. Why would Vargas be in jail if she were part of it? Wouldn't she have lied about the shooting? Or was it all part of the scam? Or maybe a double cross? Men like Vargas didn't like being crossed.

Samantha could be a murderer.

Or was she an accessory to murder?

Or things could have gone down just as she reported.

He ran his fingers through his hair. He didn't know what to think. So many unanswered questions. Part of him wanted to believe her. He couldn't forget a wealthy woman had screwed him over before. All this emotional gibberish about love and games interfered with his thinking. He had to keep his thoughts on being a cop. A cop who was sworn by duty to protect her from all harm, and he would.

Along with those thoughts eating away at his gut,

this feeling Mike was up to something wouldn't let go. Maybe the captain wanted him to pick up or check out something at her house for the department. Damn. Life would be a lot easier if he knew the truth.

****

At dusk, they pulled into a place with a bright orange and green neon sign advertising cabins. Nick registered and was unlocking the door to the cabin furthest away and out of sight of the main road within minutes of their arrival. With gun drawn, he slipped into the room with Samantha inches from his backside still hugging her backpack. At his okay, she took a deep breath and choked on the strong smell of roses. The faded wallpaper swaying in the breeze in the left corner caught her eye first. Everything was old and faded, including the bedspread on the one and only bed. She stopped.

"I'm not sleeping with you."

Nick arched a brow.

"This just isn't…proper."

Nick couldn't stop the roar of laughter that bubbled from him. "Not proper? What a thing to say to your husband."

"You're not—"

"Tut. Tut." He nodded in the direction of the office. "How would it look to that nice old couple if I didn't sleep with my wife?"

"I will not now, nor will I ever sleep with you. Or be your—anything." Samantha straightened and raised her chin.

"Never? That's a long time." Nick cocked an eyebrow while his gaze bounced back and forth from the bed to Samantha. "I'm good. Damned good."

Oh, yes. She was sure of it. She knew he was trying to get a reaction out of her. And he had succeeded. She could feel the heat of his innuendo flowing through her. Keeping calm was a battle, but she managed to look unaffected. Or hoped she did.

She strolled to the window and opened it wide. She needed to get rid of the rose odor *and* lower her rising temperature. Was that her skin sizzling? What an idiot. She actually looked to be sure. Unwilling to face him head on, she glanced over her shoulder. She let her gaze travel from his head to his feet and back again.

"That's your opinion."

He laughed once again as he strolled toward her. She braced herself for his nearness. Once he got in her personal space, he leaned down to whisper in her ear.

"What's mine against millions?"

Oh, gosh. Oh, gosh. His warm breath on the side of her face made her nerves do a slaphappy tap dance and awakened those blessed butterflies in her stomach. She fought to control her reaction. With that lone bed looming on the other side of the room, she must maintain command of her emotions. She waited for her well-practiced control to slip in before she spoke.

"Living in your fantasy world again, O'Reilly?"

"It's no fantasy, *Mrs. O'Reilly.*"

"Don't let this 'marriage' go to your head." Samantha looked down at his male parts. "Or to any other area."

A slow sexy smile crept across his face. "I could light your fire."

She turned to face him. "No, thank you." She had no doubts about his abilities. That was the problem.

"You sure know how to crush a man." Nick tried to

look crestfallen but chuckled instead.

"Some men need it." She pointed to the well-worn faded chocolate lounge chair. "You can sleep there."

"I'll flip you for the bed." Nick pulled a quarter from his pocket and tossed it in the air. "Heads you win—"

She grabbed it in mid-flight. "I don't gamble."

"Sorehead."

"I'm taking a bath." Still clutching her backpack, she headed for the bathroom.

"Need me to wash your back?" he called after her.

"I can manage." She slammed the bathroom door and started fanning herself. The man was overflowing with testosterone. His muffled laughter made her smile, but she couldn't erase the vision he'd painted in her head. She chastised herself for having sexual thoughts about a man who thrived on danger. This Chadwick wouldn't travel that road again.

****

Nick propped himself up against the headboard on the bed. Going a couple rounds with her worked for him. He tried to break that damn proper attitude of hers. But Sam had given it back to him. He liked that about her. All joking aside, he needed to keep his head on straight and do his job, or they both might not see tomorrow.

An hour went by before the bathroom door opened. She entered the room wearing the same jeans outfit she'd worn all day. Her hair fell in ringlets around a face glowing from a fresh scrubbing.

Sexy and beautiful. Thoughts like that could get him in trouble. She could also be a rich babe who might have been involved in her husband's murder. That possibility cooled his libido faster than a bucket of ice dumped in his shorts.

"I don't have any clean clothes." She looked down at her outfit. "They aren't even mine."

"We'll buy some tomorrow, but no designer stuff." He pushed himself off the bed and stared at her. "Listen. It's going to be tough going the next two weeks."

"I realize that."

"Ritzy places aren't on our agenda either."

Samantha looked around the room. "Is this an example?"

He nodded. She let out a big sigh and sat on the edge of the bed looking as dejected as his dog when left behind.

"I wish this were over, and I could go home."

"Me too, but we have to live with what we're dealt." The look in her eyes made him want to reassure her that everything would be okay, but he couldn't guarantee a thing. Better to have her spitting fireballs than wallowing in defeat. He grabbed her hand. "Come on."

"We just got here. Where are we going?"

"I've got to check in with my captain."

"You go. I'm ready for bed." She tried to tug her hand free.

"Remember? Where I go, you go." She glared at him. "I saw a phone by the office." He tugged at her hand and she stood. "It's just a short walk."

"I don't need you dragging me."

"Then let's hustle."

Sputtering, she grabbed her bag and stepped outside.

"Why don't you have a cell phone like the rest of the world?"

"Easy to trace." They reached the phone and Nick placed his call, lounging against the phone booth. Samantha sat in a lawn chair on the office porch clutching her backpack to her chest—again. What treasure did it hold?

"Bianco," the captain roared.

"I take it your wife is still in California?"

"Nick?"

"In the flesh."

"Where the hell have you been? I've been going crazy waiting for you to check in."

"It's only." Nick glanced at his watch. "Five o'clock there. What's the big deal?"

"I've been sick with worry."

"Why? What's happened?" Nick straightened giving Bianco his full attention. "The decoy worked, didn't it?" Except for that possible tail from the airport, no one had followed them. He had made sure of it. "Talk to me."

"It worked without a hitch."

"And?" Nick pulled on his earlobe.

"Lucy's been shot. She's okay. A shoulder wound."

Nick cursed. He'd known the risk, but Lucy was a good cop.

"Gus and Lucy arrived in Chicago as scheduled. Thought they had lost their tail. Stopped to eat outside Chicago. The hit happened in the parking lot on their way out. Gus tackled her or…"

"You say they lost their tail?"

"Gus is positive."

"Then how did they find them?" He ran his fingers through his hair.

"That's the million-dollar question. But I'm glad you got Mrs. Thorne away clean."

"That was the plan." Lucy getting shot wasn't.

"Did you make the rendezvous point okay?"

"Yeah." Nick fingered his lobe. "I need to get going. I'll be in touch."

"Watch yourself out there."

"Always." Nick returned the phone to its cradle.

Samantha stood and walked toward him. "What's wrong?"

He noticed she twisted her hands together when nerves ate at her. They were working up a good sweat right now.

"At first light, we're out of here." He started walking back to the cabin. "Lucy was shot today."

"Oh, my God." Samantha stopped and stared at Nick. "Is she d-dead?"

Nick saw her knees give way and grabbed her around the waist. "Take it easy. She's okay." He hurried her back to the cabin. Once inside, she sat on the bed, while Nick closed the window and stood nearby checking the area.

"I've been so wrapped up in my problems, I never dreamed anyone else would be hurt." She buried her face in her hands.

"No one is blaming you." Not him, at least.

She lowered her hands. "I am. I never dreamed Lucy might get killed in my place."

"She didn't." Nick repeated what captain had told him. By the time he finished, tears were running down Samantha's cheeks. She pulled at the jacket she was wearing. "This is Lucy's."

"Lucy knew the risk when she became a cop."

"That doesn't make it right." Samantha wiped at the tears with her finger.

"Now you can understand why we have to take every possible precaution. These jokers are serious and can strike any time, any place."

"We have to stop these men. They can't get away with killing and injuring people."

"Who said the shooter was a man?"

Samantha jerked her gaze to meet his. "You mean a woman could have done this?"

He nodded. "Now let's get some rest. We're traveling far away from here tomorrow."

Chapter 5

Nick couldn't sleep. Being relegated to this piece of junk Samantha mistakenly referred to as a lounge chair didn't add to a man's comfort. His back ached. His nerves were rattled. He pulled the wooden handle to release the chair and leaned back. A cracking sound echoed in the room. Not daring to move, he lay there like a mummy stored in a tomb. One glance told him sleeping beauty hadn't heard a thing.

Sometimes he wished his mother hadn't been so good at teaching him manners. He'd been in trouble ever since he saw Sam's skimpy silk peach panties and matching bra decorating the shower rod. She lay there comfy and getting some Z's, while he kept picturing her naked under her pink T-shirt and jeans. It took every bit of willpower he had not to join her.

Dawn arrived at last. Nick had been ready to roll for hours. Samantha looked so peaceful, he hated to wake her, but he didn't want to hang around here any longer than necessary.

He tapped her feet. "Rise and shine, sleepyhead. We've got miles to cover."

She jumped upright, rubbing her eyes. "What?"

Nick's gaze shot to her pointed nipples poking against her top. His body reacted. Damn. "Get dressed. You've got fifteen minutes," he growled.

"I am dressed."

"I like you better with no bra." He gave a silent sigh of relief when she yanked the covers over her luscious breasts. Couldn't she have chosen something made of burlap?

"What time is it?" She glanced toward the window.

"Time to go." Thank you, God.

"But it's still dark outside." She lay back down, turned on her side and covered her head with the blanket mumbling, "Wake me at noon."

He yanked her blankets off.

She shrieked.

"It's noon. We're leaving in ten."

"Fine."

Nick slammed the door, glad for the brisk morning air.

****

Late that afternoon, they stopped at a local discount store. Samantha headed for the ladies' clothes, Nick trailing behind her in a slow stroll. She stopped to look at dresses and wrinkled her nose. She'd never in her life bought clothes off-the-rack.

"You aren't going to one of your society balls." He walked over to a rack of jeans. He grabbed a pair and held it up to her. Then he threw it and three more pairs into the cart. "These will be more practical."

"I don't wear"—she ran her gaze the length of the pants and added—"*Jeans*. It's not dignified." She grabbed the jeans to return them to the rack.

"You're wearing them now." He yanked them out of her hands and tossed them into the shopping cart. "Now, for some tops."

Samantha stood with her arms crossed, her backbone straight, glaring at him, praying for a chance to ditch this arrogant man.

He ignored her and held up a very low-cut emerald top. Looking at it, Nick raised and lowered his eyebrows a couple of times. "Matches your eyes. We definitely want this one." He tossed the revealing top in the cart.

"You can't expect me to wear that…that thing. I'd be embarrassed," she said waving her hands at the green object.

He put his hand on his heart. "My heart's doing flips picturing your curvy body in this sexy thing."

"Your heart will be flipping a long time before I wear such a flimsy garment." The man was a degenerate. Yet, his approval of her figure sent a warm feeling racing through her. "If you insist on picking out my clothing, get it done." They would only be part of her wardrobe for two weeks anyway.

Nick gave her a huge smile. Drat the man.

After picking out her clothes and some for himself, he said, "You can get your own shampoo and the…unmentionables."

"Gee. Thanks." Her words dripping with sarcasm.

"Just being a good husband."

She ignored him and headed for the toiletries. He chuckled. Samantha smiled to herself.

Knowing he examined every item she chose, she managed to find several full-styled granny panties she wouldn't wear in her worst nightmare.

Nick grabbed them all with one big hand. "You plan on wearing these under those hip-hugging jeans?"

"Of course. Why?" She picked up another one to examine.

"No reason." Nick threw the ones he held in his

hand back on the shelf. He took one pair and held it up to the jeans.

"Oh," she said, her act of rebellion backfiring. She found several more to his liking and tossed them in the cart. The thought that he would be guessing which one she wore under her jeans each day gave her a teasing kind of thrill.

A tall teenage gangly guy, all skinny arms and legs, greeted them at the cash register. He eyed Samantha with instant lust. He fumbled with several items before reaching for her unmentionables. His face turned crimson staring at her. She smiled at him in understanding and whipped out her credit card. "This should take care of everything."

Nick snatched it out of the cashier's hand, mumbling for only Samantha's ears, "What the hell are you doing?"

The cashier threw an angry glare at him. "It's okay, son." He put his arm around a surly Samantha and drew her close. "We just eloped, and my wife keeps forgetting I'm the bread winner in this family now." He smiled down at her, but his wide-opened eyes were sending another message. "Isn't that right, dear?"

Between tight lips Samantha said, "Yes, dear."

The teenager gave him a knowing wink and finished the order with the cash Nick handed him.

Back by the truck, loaded down with everything Nick thought they needed, Samantha got in. She stared straight ahead and remained silent. This know-it-all cop had tons of nerve. Choosing her clothes! Funny, the excitement he seemed to get from doing so touched her heart. Yet, he was just playing a role. She must always remember that fact.

Nick jumped into the driver's seat. Before he started the engine, he turned to her. "Come on. Don't be in a snit. I never bought clothes for a woman before."

Samantha turned to face him. "It's been years since anyone thought to pick out my clothes. Not that I would let them, but…" The intimacy of it all warmed her. She covered her feelings by saying, "I don't usually wear jeans." Remembering Lucy, she looked down at her legs. "These aren't even mine."

"Listen, Sam. We don't know what's ahead of us. Running in pants is easier than trying to move fast in a dress."

"It's just that—"

He smiled. "You'll get to love them. I do."

"We'll see." She stared out the window.

****

Nick drove over the state border into northern Arkansas a couple hours later. Taking the less traveled routes and back tracking had cost them time. They weren't in a rush as long as they got to their preplanned destination each night.

The captain insisted on having nightly rendezvous points. Nick disagreed. He'd never forget the hotheaded argument that followed. Sure, the captain needed to be in control, but it reeked of a chance for a possible setup to happen. And that put Nick on full alert.

He didn't think they were being followed, but being watchful wouldn't hurt. Caution and instinct had kept him alive for thirty-four years. He wasn't about to give up on them now.

That evening, Nick pulled into a small run-down two-story motel outside of Fayetteville, Arkansas. Nick could have sworn a worm slithered up his spine. He shuddered. Everything seemed in place. His gut told him otherwise. His gut never lied.

"Is there a reason why we've been sitting here for the last several minutes with the motor running?" Samantha looked around the parking lot.

Those were the first words she'd spoken since her snit earlier. "No. Just thinking." He turned the engine off. "Come on. Let's get registered in this dump."

Samantha looked around. "If you detest it so, why don't we find something more suitable?"

"Can't. Not part of the plan."

"And what, pray tell, might that be?"

"To keep you safe." He slipped out of the truck, his gaze taking in everything around him. "Let's go inside. I'll do the talking." They signed in under the name of VanEver and made their way to the room he'd requested. Corner. Second floor. Two windows. He didn't want some jerk jumping in or shooting at them through a ground floor window. Plus, he wanted a good visual of the outside. He unlocked the door and motioned for her to stand back while he checked it out.

"It's clear." Nick motioned for Samantha to come in.

Samantha looked around as she stepped into the room, her disapproval evident by her upturned nose. The wallpaper wasn't falling off the walls, but the green paint had seen a better day. A picture of a black cat playing with a string hung crooked on the wall.

"So, what's the verdict?"

"At least it has two beds."

"That it does." *Thank God.* He still had a kink in his back from the broken-down piece of junk at the other place. Sniffing her scent and being in such close quarters with her all day didn't lessen his urges any. The next problem would be sleeping night after night in the same room with her and keeping his lust under control. How in hell had he gotten this job? He wanted nothing to do with a greenback-loaded babe, especially one so attractive in many ways.

"Which bed do you want?" Samantha set her backpack on the desk and turned to face Nick.

"I'll take the one nearest the door." That put him between her and any unwanted visitors.

"Are we ordering room service?" Samantha's stomach chose that moment to rumble.

Nick shrugged. "No room service."

"I thought all hotels served food in their rooms."

"See, now there's the rub." He scratched his chin.

"What do you mean?" Samantha took a step toward him.

"This is a motel, not a hotel."

"Oh." She thought for a moment. "I've never been in a motel. We always stayed—"

"In high class joints." He couldn't hide his disgust. He knew he was acting like a low-class snob, but she was right. He did have something against the wealthy, but it didn't have anything to do with this gal and her dough.

"Well, yes. We usually stayed in five-star hotels but—"

"The Ritz isn't in a cop's budget." And never would be.

"It seems my social status is more of a problem to you than yours is to me." Samantha raised an eyebrow.

"Now why would you say that?" Nick raised his brow, too.

"Who was she, Detective?"

"Who was who?" Nick wasn't about to answer that one.

"The wealthy woman who hurt you. Was she your wife? A girlfriend?" She stared at him, waiting for a response.

"Snooping, Mrs. Thorne?"

She ignored his question. "What did she do? Leave you for another man?"

"Yep. Definitely snooping." He grinned to cover the hurt he fought to keep buried. He never talked about his ex-fiancée. Ever.

Samantha shrugged. "Maybe someday you'll let me or someone help you remove the pain from your heart."

"Now you're a shrink too?" Sarcasm dripped from each word.

"Along with being trained to be a wealthy man's wife, I obtained a degree in psychology."

"Figures. Close your notepad, Doc. You won't need it on this trip." Nick stared at her, his legs spread and his arms crossed over his chest. Snow can fall at the equator before he'd confide in her. He'd always kept his life his own. Nick O'Reilly needed no one, especially a *psychologist*. "Best you remember that, Mrs. Edward Chadwick-Thorne."

Samantha gaze softened while she stared at him for a moment. He felt his blood heat to the boiling point. "I don't need your damn pity either."

"You won't get it, but my offer still stands." She grabbed her backpack and headed toward the bathroom. "I've always dined at seven." Samantha looked at her watch. "It is now ten past. I shall be out shortly. Then I intend to have dinner with or without a bodyguard."

All Nick could do was stand there, wondering what in hell had just happened. He felt like pond scum inside and out. The lady had a kind heart, and though overwhelmed with her own problems, she offered to help him out. What did he do? Good Old Nick O'Reilly got his Irish temper up and put her down.

"It's my life. I don't need a shrink," he muttered to the empty room. He cursed. Captain Bianco would have reminded him that he should've outgrown the rotten street kid attitude years ago. Maybe he hadn't gotten far from his roots after all.

****

They ate dinner in silence. Nick chewed on his shrimp while she nibbled on her stuffed haddock. Samantha took every opportunity to study him without his knowledge. What a lonely man. Oh, he worked hard to cover it up, but it didn't take a college degree to recognize a man who had been terribly hurt by a wealthy woman. It was none of her business, of course, but it did arouse her curiosity. Maybe he'd take her advice and talk to her. She could see her mother giving up her Tuesday afternoon bridge game first, something she had been doing without fail for over thirty years. She saw little chance of that happening now or in the near future. And why should she care? They'd never see each other again after the trial. She didn't know if that pleased her or not.

After a dinner eaten in tense silence, Nick rose and tossed some bills on the table. He motioned for her to follow him. Not wanting to start an argument, she did as he ordered. Once outside, he took her arm and hurried her toward the motel. When she stumbled in her haste, she yanked her arm from his grip and stopped moving.

"What *is* your problem?"

"We need to get inside."

"Why? The place is deserted." She looked around, wondering if she'd missed something. Or someone. "I was thinking of taking a walk."

"Out of the question." Nick took her arm again and pulled her toward the hotel.

Samantha opened her mouth to protest at the same moment he cursed and shoved her behind a nearby tree.

"What are you doing?" she sputtered, trying to push him away with one hand while grasping her backpack to her chest with the other. Then she saw the gun in his hand. She gasped. A shiver of fear shook her.

"Stay close to the tree. I saw a flash."

"A g-gun?"

"Might be just a reflection."

The squeeze he gave her shoulder did nothing to reassure her. She kept swallowing to keep her dinner down. Nick, on the other hand, checked everything in sight. When he holstered his gun and smiled at her, she would have collapsed from relief if he hadn't grabbed her shoulders.

"You okay?"

"Yes." No. She had been shaking in her boots, but she wouldn't let him know.

"Take a look, Sam." Nick turned her and pointed toward the cars zooming down the nearby highway. "I saw light reflecting off that silver sign." With a little sheepish grin, he added, "Guess I'm a little jumpy."

"That's okay. We both are and with good reason." Better he be cautious, though her nerves were now strung tighter than piano wires and the food she had just eaten churned in her stomach.

"No strolling tonight."

"I heartedly agree. Shall we?" Samantha motioned with her head toward the motel.

"By all means."

Once they were back in the room, Nick pulled a gun from the holster strapped to his leg.

"Here." He held the gun out to her. "Keep this."

She thought her eyes would pop out of her head. Was he crazy? Samantha Chadwick put her hands on a gun? Never. She stepped back, shaking her head. "No. Not me."

"You might need it." Nick held the pistol closer to her.

She twisted away from the weapon. "You've got to be kidding."

"Am I laughing?"

"But I don't know the first thing about—"

"I'll give you a crash course." He proceeded to instruct her on how to load, aim and fire his weapon. "The safety action on this Glock 26 is automatic. It's on until you pull the trigger and turns back on at the release of the trigger. Safety is built into the gun making it real easy." He held the pistol out to her.

"No. I don't want to even touch it." She shivered. "I hate guns." They kill people. One killed Edward.

"It might save your life. Now take it and repeat what I just showed you."

After protesting several times and with shaking hands, Samantha took hold of the black handle with her index finger and her thumb. The weight caused her hand to drop a couple inches. She dangled the gun an arms-length in front of her noting how warm it felt from Nick's body heat. A tingle ran up her arm.

He chuckled. "It won't bite. Remember, the safety is always on."

"This isn't a good idea. I could never shoot anyone. Here." She stepped toward him. "Take it back."

"No." Nick moved away from her.

"But I don't know how to use it. Nor do I want to learn."

"For now, just learn the basics. We'll stop and target practice the first chance we get."

Her mouth dropped open. "Target practice?"

He put his hand to his ear. "Is there an echo in here?"

"Why do you want me to do this? Edward was—"

"Just stick the piece in that satchel of yours." He ran his fingers through his hair.

"What's really wrong?" Were Vargas' gunmen around? Why was he behaving this way? She didn't like this gun thing one little bit. Guns scared her. Even more so since she had been shot in the arm and Edward had been killed.

He shrugged. "Nothing. Everything."

"Is your feeling that strong?" *Please say no.*

"Yeah." He rubbed the back of his neck.

"Okay. But I'll never use…*the piece.*"

"We'll see." Nick motioned toward her bag.

To appease him, Samantha dropped it into her backpack. That piece of metal could rust away in there for all she cared.

****

Sleep hadn't come easily to Samantha. Nick's quiet snore in the other bed and her wandering thoughts had kept her alert most of the night. There was something about him that attracted her. Could it be his bad-boy attitude? Her mother had warned her against his type, but she did enjoy arguing with him.

Edward hadn't sparred with her at all. He'd turned serious and grouchy after their marriage. Maybe that's why her feelings for him never got a chance to grow.

What would making love be like to a man she truly loved?

Mother had preached that it was her wifely duty to lie with her husband to help him obtain his "manly release" whenever he desired it. Samantha felt sorry for her father if her mother treated him that way all these years. Hadn't she treated Edward in a similar way? Not in the beginning. After a while, he seemed preoccupied and had lost his passion for her. Why couldn't he have been more of a man's man like Nick? Why compare the two anyway? One was dead and the other would be out of her life in less than two weeks.

"You okay?" Nick stood fully clothed in the shadows near the front window.

"Yes. I'm fine." When had he gotten up? She must have dozed off at some point.

"You've been staring at the ceiling and using that backpack for life support for the last ten minutes."

It's a good thing he didn't know what the bag contained or what thoughts twirled in her head. Nick worked hard at being a cop. He used his badge as a barrier to keep everyone away. For pure professional curiosity, she'd love to know more about the lady who'd hurt him. It could be for no other reason. Her money stood in his way and his job in hers. At the moment, his tenseness was catching.

"What's happening? What is making you worry?" she asked, sitting up in bed.

"Not sure."

"Talk to me, please." That chill took another trip up her spine. The shakes returned.

He checked his watch. "We need to get moving."

Nick paced the small area, pulling on his earlobe, something he did when he was concerned. Samantha stared at him, waiting for an answer.

"It's my gut."

"Do you want an antacid?" She unzipped her backpack.

He grinned and shook his head. "It's not like that."

Nick's eagle eyes bore into her. She fought not to cringe under their direct appraisal. When he pulled on that right lobe again, she knew he battled with himself about what to tell her.

"I've got this feeling. It's been there all night." He stopped by the front window, peeked around the curtain, and did a slow surveillance. "I've checked here a dozen times, but I never see anything unusual."

"That's a good sign, isn't it?"

"Yes and no."

"What does that mean?" She threw back the covers and crawled off the bed.

"Yes. They haven't found us. No. They may be just out of sight, waiting."

That's all it took to get her moving toward the bathroom. "I'll be right out." Five minutes later, she stepped into the room, dressed, and braced for whatever came their way. "Please be careful." She gathered her belongings and stuck them in the small tote Nick had purchased.

"Worried about me, Sam?" He gave her a cocky grin.

She stopped what she was doing. She looked him in the eyes and said, "I'm concerned about me. The police need *me* to put Vargas behind bars for life. They get you, they'll get me. I value my life and want to stay alive."

Nick stiffened. His gray eyes bore into her once again. The anger flowing from him was palatable. Then his whole demeanor changed. He shut down. Hardened.

As soon as the words left her mouth, she wanted to take them back. How selfish could she get? He had been doing a splendid job of keeping her safe. To reward him, she had given him a verbal stab in the back. "I'm sorry. I didn't mean it. I'm just nervous about this whole thing."

"Don't be. I needed the reminder."

"What does that mean?" She was afraid she already knew but wanted him to say it. But he ignored the question.

"Stay put. I'll check outside." He drew his gun and checked through the peephole in the door. Then he unlocked the door, opened it a crack and looked out.

Satisfied, he stepped outside. A man leaped at him, knocking Nick's gun from his hand.

"Shut the door," Nick shouted.

She froze. Then jumped into action. The door crashed against the wall. A man dressed in black, his face covered with a ski mask, rushed into the room. He grabbed for her. She sidestepped him and swung her backpack at his head.

"Humph!" he moaned, falling back.

She ran for the door. The man recovered fast. He

latched onto her arm and pulled. Pain shot into her shoulder. She screamed. "Don't you dare touch me," she yelled, using her free hand to punch him wherever she could reach.

"Bitch," he yelled, grabbing her other hand.

The man was strong. She kicked at him and nailed him in the shin. He swore at her. But his hold remained firm.

"Hellcat," he growled. Then slapped her hard on the side the head.

Samantha saw stars floating before her eyes. Her ear was ringing and her face stung. She fought with everything she had to stay conscious. She would have fallen if his grip on her arm wasn't so fierce.

"Hold her," a gruff voice said behind her. Suddenly, a wet smelly rag was jammed in her face. She shook her head to free herself from the stench. Choking, she heard a muffled noise.

A shot?

Nick! They've killed Nick! How she wished she hadn't uttered those cruel words only moments ago. Then all went black.

Chapter 6

Samantha struggled to raise her eyelids. The sun's brightness sent hundreds of firecrackers exploding in her head. Her mouth watered. Bile burned the back of her throat. What had happened to her? Then she remembered. Nick was dead. Tears filled her eyes and rolled down her cheeks. Poor Nick. She regretted the things she had said to him. Depression settled over her, driving a dark void deep into her soul. The short length of time she had known him didn't matter. Her grief suffocated her.

Nick died protecting her.

She would never get the chance to spar with him again over nonsense. Never get the chance to feel his strong arms around her, to kiss him or make love to him. She gave herself a mental whipping. How could she be so selfish and think only of herself?

The sudden sharp turn jerked Samantha hard against the seat back. Suddenly, she realized she was lying in the back seat of a car. Her thoughts settled on one thing.

Vargas had succeeded in capturing her.

All her hopes and dreams of living free collapsed around her. Vargas would kill her once he got his murdering hands on the cross. She began to shake all over. Her heart raced. Her head throbbed with every beat. How she wished Nick were here. He'd know what to do.

Enough of this poor-me pity party. Fury replaced the fear jamming her throat. She straightened her spine. No lowlife would stop her from testifying and tossing the scum of the earth in jail. She wouldn't allow it. She'd get revenge for Nick. But how?

From her angle, she couldn't see the driver. She moved to get a better look. A swirl of dizziness grabbed her. Samantha rubbed her throbbing head. Then she realized. Her hands weren't bound. Neither were her feet. Her kidnapper couldn't be that ignorant, could he? Her backpack held a gun!

She spotted the pack on the floor and gave a silent sigh of relief. She eased her shoulders over to the edge of the seat. She reached down, found the strap and pulled the bag up to her chest. The gun and the jars were still there. She could feel them. Samantha relaxed back onto the seat.

She couldn't use the gun. Not on a living thing. But a club. That she could do. She got a good grip on the straps and waited, willing away the woozy feeling in her head.

The car stopped.

Samantha jumped up and let her bag fly. "Take that you…you murderer."

The man's hand shot up. "What the…?"

The full force of the strike bounced off the passenger's headrest and hit the arm of the driver. Then, it flew back to hit her in the head. "Oomph!" She saw stars once again. She fell against the back of the seat. What could she do now? Standing up would be impossible even if she could manage to open the door. Her abductor knew she was awake.

"What in hell are you trying to do, Sam?"

Samantha's gaze shot to the mirror. No one called her Sam but…

"Is that you, Nick?"

"What're you trying to do, kill me?" He was watching her through the rearview mirror.

"I thought you were already dead." Samantha swallowed hard. How wonderful he looked. A great sense of joy filled her. She smiled. Then laughed. "You're alive!"

Nick rubbed his arm. "No thanks to you."

"I thought you were my kidnapper."

He turned to look over his shoulder. "You crazy?"

"What was I supposed to think? I thought you were dead and some stranger had—"

"Dead? Me?" Nick shook his head. "Have you no faith, Sam?"

"Yes, but I heard a shot and thought—" She didn't want to remember. All this talk of gun shots and killing made her stomach churn.

"The worst." Nick shook his head. "Don't you think a killer would have restrained you, preventing you from doing what you just tried to do to me?"

"I wondered about that," Samantha muttered, looking out the side window. He must think her to be a brainless fool. At the moment, she felt that way.

A horn blared behind them. "Sit tight a minute."

Sit tight? What else could she do? At the moment, Samantha wished she had a different head. Closing her eyes didn't help. She sat up straight and the world settled down. Nick pulled into a parking spot at a diner. The churning in her stomach increased. "You want food?"

"It's lunch time." He stopped the car and turned to look at her. "Hey, are you okay?"

She laid her head against the seat. "A little dizzy, s'all."

"It's the drug."

"I don't tolerate them well."

"The doctor said—"

"You took me to a doctor?" She had a hard time believing he would under the circumstances.

"On the way out of town, I stopped at a clinic."

And I never knew or felt a thing.

"My. Gosh. How much dope did they give me? Is it dangerous?"

"Naw. Just enough to give you a whopper of a headache." He looked at his watch. "You'll be okay soon." He got out of the car, opened the back door, and helped her out. She staggered. He wrapped his arm around her waist to steady her. Nick smiled at her. "Ever been drunk?"

"Not really. Just feeling good s'all."

"Now you know what it feels like." Having his hard body next to hers made her shiver. "Let's get you warm." Nick drew her closer and hurried inside the diner.

The odors of frying meat made her real sick. She needed a bathroom. Instead, he hurried her to a nearby booth. Samantha sat down and looked him in the face for the first time. "I need to…Oh, My. You've got a black eye. Did—"

"Not now."

His sharp bark left her silent with her mouth hanging open, her stomach problems forgotten. She had to think of something else or she might say something she'd be sorry for in the end. Samantha turned her attention to the boxcar-like diner, willing herself to keep her mouth shut. Red and white checks predominated. The small apron on the giant woman marching toward their booth managed to reflect the decor. The waitress had to be in her fifties. She towered at least six feet with a waistline half the size of her height.

"Howdy, folks. I'm Cindy Lou." She looked Nick over from head to toe. "Wow-wee. Ain't you the stud?" Cindy Lou grabbed his chin and studied his black eye. "Mmmmm." She nodded toward Samantha. "Love touch from the missus?"

"Ran into a door." Nick moved his head, freeing his chin from her hand.

Cindy Lou turned to Samantha and eyeballed her from head to toe. "Some door."

Samantha couldn't stop a smile from tugging at her lips. *Stud*! She raised her eyebrows at him. He glared and mumbled something under his breathe.

"Trouble in paradise, handsome?" Cindy Lou asked.

"Nothing I can't handle," he said, daring her to contradict him.

Samantha decided to ignore him but couldn't help the roaring laughter going on inside her.

Cindy Lou, however, roared with laughter causing her good-sized middle to wiggle like Santa's belly in the Christmas story her father used to read to her. After she got herself under control, she turned to Samantha and clasped her hands over her heart and sighed. "Quite a catch you've landed yourself, gal."

She had never seen anyone like Cindy Lou before.

Polite waiters in black coats and ties with white towels over their arms were the norm for her. Nick grinned. He was enjoying this waitress's brassy conduct.

Now was the time for this "wife" to have her fun by turning this *inconvenient marriage* into a convenient one for her. She smiled at him and raised her left eyebrow. "Isn't my *stud* the cutest thing you ever saw?" His frown said it all.

Cindy Lou roared again. "Sure is a honey." She turned back to Nick. "Ya'll need some beef fer that eye, handsome?"

"Naw. It's okay."

She patted Nick's shoulder. "Suit yourself, *stud*. You want your poison black, leaded and strong?"

"Yep." He winked at Cindy Lou.

"And your missus?"

"Oh, but—" He stepped on her foot. She scowled at him.

"The usual, darlin'?" he interrupted, throwing daggers at her with his eyes.

"Yes, *dear*." Samantha got two raised eyebrows from him for her sarcasm. "Hot tea with lemon. Please." Cindy Lou nodded and left cackling.

"She likes you, *Stud*." This time she let the laughter burst from her lips and grabbed for her head. "Don't make me laugh. It hurts."

Nick leaned toward her. "Jealous?"

She shook her head. "Possessive of what's mine." She reached over and touched his hand. It took Nick's dark brown eyes peering deep into her soul to make her realize what she had said…and done. Based on the way her fingers were tingling, the possible truth in her words was even more jarring.

"Before you get any ideas"—she wiggled her ring finger in his face—"I'm referring to our *marriage.*"

He grabbed her hand. When he leaned over and kissed her wedding ring, her heart raced. A warming sensation ran up her arm and aroused those blessed flutters again in her stomach. He held her gaze. For a moment, she couldn't breathe. Then she remembered. This was all an act. She tried to remove her hand. He increased the pressure and rolled his eyes toward their waitress. Cindy Lou leaned against the counter watching them, wearing a knowing smile.

At last, Cindy Lou turned away and to cover her own embarrassment, Samantha said, "You can let go now, *Stud.* Your girlfriend has gone back to work." He blushed. She giggled. He grabbed his menu and hid behind it. Suddenly, her world righted. Time to order.

"What happened this morning?" she asked after their food arrived. She sipped her chicken soup, while he demolished a steak. "There were several of them."

"Only three." Nick shrugged. "Easy cuff." She let her gaze roam the bruises on his face. He touched his eye. "All part of the job."

"And?" She knew he wouldn't tell her how he'd outmaneuvered them, but she'd let it go for now.

"The local sheriff threw them in jail."

"And the car?" She nodded toward the parking lot.

"The perps don't need it."

"Perps?"

"Perpetrators." Nick bit a piece of steak from his fork.

"You took a car belonging to *Vargas*?"

"Naw. It was rented."

"Are you crazy?" She stared at him. Had he lost his

mind? "Edward is a perfect example of what happens to a person who steals from Vargas."

And I've done the same.

The sudden realization set her back for a moment until she reminded herself she had taken the cross for protection.

Nick shrugged. "You were unconscious. We needed wheels." He chewed on his food.

She leaned back and stared at him. He'd taken a beating protecting her. No one had ever done that for her before. Something inside her jumped to life. She couldn't begin to name it, having never felt this way before. It had to be her overwhelming gratitude.

"Something wrong, Sam?"

"I'm fine. I just now realized you risked your life once again to save mine. Thank you."

"You're welcome." He studied her for a long time. "Now finish your soup." He cut a piece of steak and put it in his mouth, motioning for her to eat, too.

"Aren't you going to make some comment about doing your job?"

"Nope. Eat. We've got to get moving." He cut another piece of meat and stuffed it in his mouth.

"You think we're still being followed." Nick's lack of a response told her what she needed to know. She looked out the window into the parking lot, searching for she knew not what. Maybe gunmen sat in their cars waiting to shoot her like they did Lucy. She didn't like it that people were getting hurt because of her. Vargas would pay for murdering her husband and hurting the people protecting her. Samantha would make sure of it.

****

Within a half-hour later, Nick drove down the

84

interstate once again. A smile tugged at his mouth remembering Cindy Lou's loud, "Ya'll come back, Stud," when they left the diner. He liked her and had left a hefty tip. Her crazy antics made Samantha lose most of her pallor. Nick enjoyed watching Samantha's reactions. He would bet she'd never seen anything like that old gal.

For a time back there, he would've sworn Sam was jealous. Or had she gotten into their role-playing for real? Had he? Naw. It'd been just an act for Cindy Lou. He wasn't Sam's type, nor she his. He frowned. They had connected. Being a couple felt right. Yet, they still had that I'm-loaded-and-you're-not thing between them.

Nick glanced over at the beautiful woman riding beside him. Samantha's silence bothered him. Not a peep had squeaked out of her since they'd left the diner. She still hung on to that pack of hers like a lifeline. He wondered what could be going on in her gorgeous head.

"They know where we are, don't they?"

"Yep." Worrying. That's what she had been doing.

"How? You've only talked to your captain."

"They know our schedule." He wondered once again if the mole in the department was his partner. Mike helped make the plan. So did his boss, but he trusted the captain. He couldn't help but wonder who else knew too. Vargas' men knew where they were every night. Coincidence? He'd bet his badge they knew their Plan A. He'd have to come up with a Plan B. He shrugged his shoulders. "How else could they find us?"

"Who knows the schedule besides you?" Samantha turned to face him.

He looked at her. "Don't let it worry you."

"Is that a 'none of your business' statement?"

Nick's gaze returned to the road, and he said nothing.

"I don't think we should go to our next scheduled motel," Samantha suggested.

"Nope." Hell no.

"You've already decided this?"

He snickered at her stern tone. "Yep."

"Are you going to let me in on your plan?" When he didn't answer, she slapped her backpack. "You are very frustrating."

"So I'm told." He gave her a big smile.

She mumbled something he couldn't hear and stared straight ahead in silence.

Nick was acting like a jerk for a reason. The idea forming in his head would take money. Lots of money.

"Hey, Sam?" She ignored him. "Got any money?"

He saw her fists tightened around her backpack. Did she have money in that pouch? Lots of money? That would explain the tight hold she always had on that satchel. "Well. Do you?"

"What I have or don't have is none of your business, *Detective*."

"Great. We're back to name calling again." Man, she could be snippy when she wanted to be. "So, how much ya got?"

Samantha turned toward him. "Why are you asking?"

"We need a home." Not a mansion, either.

"I already have one of my own."

"Yep. A real ritzy place, too." Damn. Why the dig? Her social status wasn't any of his business.

"Thank you. I'm correct in thinking that we can't go back there now, right?"

"Got it in one."

"Then why do you want to buy a house?"

"I don't."

Samantha turned farther around once again to face him. "But you just said—"

"We need cover." Nick glanced at her, anticipating her reaction. "We could pitch a tent in the woods."

Eyes bulging, she croaked, "Pitch a *what*?"

He loved the expression on her face. "A tent. You know, those canvas things campers use to keep out of the weather."

"You're joking." He shook his head. "You have to be."

"They're cheap and easy to transport. Just think how comfy it will be with just the two of us all snuggled together in cozy sleeping bags, side-by-side on pine needles to soften the nice hard ground." He took a deep breath and sighed. "I like a soft bed, don't you?"

The look she gave him would have made snow fall in the Sonora Desert. He covered his grin with a cough.

"Not in this lifetime nor the next." Her grip tightened on the bag and her chin went up.

"Come on, Sam, be reasonable. What other choice do we have?" They had one other choice.

"I'm not sleeping in a...tent with you or anyone else." She turned back to face the road.

Nick felt good. It always pleased him when he got a reaction out of her. He'd had his fun. Time to get serious.

"Would a *mobile* home, otherwise known as an

RV, better suit your highness?" He sure as hell would like it better.

Samantha's gaze shot to Nick's. "An RV?"

"You know, one of those tin boxes on wheels."

She frowned. "I know what an RV is."

"Of course. They make nice toys for the rich." Why couldn't he keep his mouth shut?

"Gee, I guess I missed owning one of those." She pretended to write on something. "But I'll add it to my list."

"Glad to help." Nick went silent to let her think about his suggestion for a while. Her next question was a surprise.

"An RV will give us more flexibility, won't it?"

"We can camp anywhere." At least he had her thinking.

"Are you serious?"

"Yep. Roaring fires. Moonlight walks. Bears."

"Now you are kidding." Samantha shivered at the thought.

Amused, he added, "Campers enjoy them." He slipped a glance her way. "Or so I've heard."

"You've heard?" She studied him for a moment. "Have you ever been camping?"

"Hell, no. I'm city born and raised." Caught by his own words, he grinned.

"Then how will we know what to do? The closest I've been to a forest is the city park." She hugged herself.

"Life is full of new experiences." Where did the idea of camping come from in the first place? He didn't know the first or last thing about living in the rough. Heck, he didn't know how to drive an RV either. Guess the time to learn had arrived.

"You're trying to scare me."

"Now why would I do that?" He worked hard not to smile. He fell silent. His thoughts turned serious. How to get an RV? Stealing it was out. Renting one was their best chance. "We need a lot of hard cash. Credit cards are too easy to trace." Nick's thoughts flowed from his lips. "Where in hell can I find that much green stuff?" He unwrapped a Tootsie Roll with one hand and stuffed it in his mouth.

Staring straight ahead once again, she said, "I have some money."

He choked on his candy. Coughed. Did she really have lots of greenbacks with her? "How much?"

She told him. He whistled. "No wonder you've got a stranglehold on your backpack. Or are you keeping something for Vargas, too?"

Samantha felt the blood rush from her face. She didn't realize she had such a death grip on her bag. If he knew the truth, he wouldn't be so smug. Yes, she had a cross belonging to Vargas. No, she would never hold it *for* him. If she could mail the letter to Vargas, all these attempts on her life would cease. "Why in this world or the next would I keep anything for him?"

He glanced at her. "You tell me."

"For goodness sake, Vargas killed my husband. He is trying very hard to do the same to me."

"Did you help him?"

"What? You think I—"

"Everyone's a suspect."

"Thank you. Now I know what you think of me." Knowing where she stood with him made a huge difference.

"All part of the job." Nick pulled on his ear. "Do you usually carry that much bread with you?"

"Bread? Oh, you mean money." He raised a brow. "No. This is the first time."

"And your plans were to…?"

"Provide for an emergency." Such as, running away from him the first chance she got.

"We got us one hell of an emergency, Sam."

She leaned back in the seat and sighed. There would be no chance for her to escape without the money. Samantha began to doubt that she could survive on her own. He had saved her life many times already.

He stepped hard on the gas pedal driving her against the seat.

"What are you doing?"

He shrugged. "What else? We're going to spend your money."

****

By five o'clock that evening near Fayetteville, Arkansas, Nick had rented a renovated ivory and tan RV for two weeks. The dealer claimed the camper would sleep four. She spotted two beds, one double and one bunk. That's what they would need. Now wasn't the time to think further on sleeping arrangements. She had a letter to mail.

Samantha looked around for a mailbox. She spotted one on a nearby corner and wandered toward it. Nick was listening to the salesman's demonstration on the "how-to-do" features of the RV, filling the water tanks and whatever else he needed to know. She glanced around to make sure he wasn't watching. Then, she slipped the letter in the open slot. Once Vargas got the letter, he would ease off on the death threats.

Having the cross had to be her safety net. Or so she hoped.

She stepped back from the mailbox and realized what she had just done. Without warning, the shakes hit her hard. Suppose the letter didn't work as she planned? Vargas may be more determined than ever. The letter could lead him straight to her. Why didn't she think this through first? Could she retrieve the letter from the box? She peeked into the opening.

"Lose something?" Nick whispered near her ear.

"Oh. My. Gosh!" She jerked back into a hard chest. His big strong hands grabbed her shoulders to steady her. A warm feeling fluttered through her.

"Mailing something?"

Those warm feelings froze. Guilt filled her. Thank goodness her back was to him. She shied away from his touch. Admitting to mailing a letter would bring on more questions than she wanted to answer. Questions would lead to the cross and where it was hidden. She knew she should tell him, but the street corner didn't seem to be the place.

"I wish you wouldn't sneak up on me like that," she snapped. Had he seen her mail the letter?

"Why so jumpy? Never seen a mailbox before?"

"Don't be silly. Are we ready to leave?" Samantha hurried toward the RV relieved to have been able to change the subject. She sent up a silent prayer that the letter would protect her and not bring Vargas running straight to her.

Chapter 7

After leaving the rental car at a rest area outside of town, Samantha and Nick headed toward Arkansas in the RV.

"Do you know how to drive this thing?" She motioned to the steering wheel.

"What do you think I am? An adolescent on a permit?"

"Just checking."

It didn't take long for Nick's inexperience in driving an RV to become obvious. The first intersection they stopped at, he did a lot of grinding of the gears. Sitting in the cross traffic he couldn't get it in the right gear. Horns were blowing all around them. He cursed with every try that failed.

"What did you say about an adolescent permit?" She had a hard time keeping a straight face, but laughed hard on the inside. This macho man thought he could do anything. She had to give him credit for trying.

The glare he aimed at her could have sent her flying around the world twice. He cursed again and tried once more to get the RV moving.

"All those drivers are getting angrier by the minute."

"So? I can…" In that instant, he found the right gear and they jerked forward. "See. That wasn't hard." A big smile crossed his face.

"Congratulations!" She couldn't help the chuckle that burst from her throat. This sure was a determined man.

By the time he pulled into a public campsite in the Boston Mountains in Arkansas the sun had disappeared. Samantha breathed a sigh of relief. Maybe he would have better luck parking this monster. She could only hope so at this point.

Two hours later in the shadows of darkness, Nick cursed. "I won't let this stump me."

"What did you say?" She worked hard at holding the flashlight steady.

"I'll level this piece of tin on wheels or else." He went back to raising the jack.

Samantha grinned to herself. He'd been doing just that for over an hour. A twig snapped in the woods. She looked into the dark wooded area surrounding their camp. Her heart was pounding hard in her throat while she kept telling herself she had nothing to fear. She waved the flashlight toward the noise. She studied the trees but saw nothing. She wouldn't have been surprised to see Big Foot emerge at any moment.

"Would you stop pretending to be a northern light and hold the damn light down here?" He pointed to the leveling jack. "I don't have night vision."

He'd said the wrong thing. "Oh? A northern light, you say?" Samantha waved the flashlight, making the beams of light flash in the trees to cover her need to search for the trespasser. The sound of breaking twigs came again. She aimed the light in the direction of the noise. Nothing. It was too soon for Vargas to be near, she reasoned. Was it one of the bears Nick spoke of recently? Her fear and the need to get safe inside the camper increased.

"Knock it off, Sam."

She aimed the light toward him. "Are you done yet?" *Please say yes!* The darkness terrified her. She didn't know how long she could keep it together.

"No!" Nick kicked at a board under the back tire.

"Don't shout. It's not my fault this place is built on the side of a hill." The man sure could get surly when things didn't go his way. Thinking back, she realized he did have reason to be frustrated and upset.

Everything imaginable had happened. They'd thought they were lucky to get the last remaining site on the campgrounds until they discovered everything sloped. Then he put a man-sized dent in the bumper, backing into a tree. Nothing deterred a stubborn Nick O'Reilly. Not even the offer of help. Mr. First-Time-Know-It-All Camper had the gall to refuse the aid of an older, more experienced gentleman. Mr. Good Samaritan must be bent over with hysterics watching this fiasco.

"Just let it go for tonight. I'm sure we can live through one night with the RV tilted."

He glared at her. "This piece of crap *will* be level."

"Suit yourself." Whatever species prowled the woods, moved again. Samantha stepped closer to Nick. "But could you hurry it up some?" He mumbled something she couldn't hear.

Another hour passed. Nick kept his word. The RV remained tilted, but he continued his determination to win. Cold, hungry, and frightened, Samantha clicked off the switch on the light. Total darkness engulfed them.

"What the hell are you doing? Turn it back on."

"No. You can fiddle with…whatever." She waved her hand toward him. "Till sunrise, but you will do it alone." She flipped the switch back on the flashlight and headed toward the door. She shivered in the damp air. "I intend to warm myself and dine. You can do as you wish." She reached for the door handle.

"Don't. Touch. It!" Nick barked.

"I told you, I'm—"

"I heard you," he mumbled, pulling her hand away from the doorknob. "So did the whole campground."

"Humph!" She yanked her hand away from his.

"If you so much as wiggle the door, this contraption will head for the trees."

"Then fix it. I'm going inside." He grumbled about pigheaded women. She bit her tongue to squelch her giggle. The old cliché, "It takes one to know one," came to mind.

After much grumbling and complaining, he removed the jacks and then blocked the wheels. "I hope you've got one leg shorter than the other because you're going to need it." Nick's mood had not improved.

"My legs are perfectly normal, thank you."

"There's nothing normal about them," he grumbled.

"I beg your pardon?" She stiffened her spine and turned to face him.

"You got great legs and you know it."

Samantha opened her mouth to speak. All coherent thought escaped her. It was the second time Nicholas O'Reilly had complimented her. He'd been simple and gruff with delivery, but nice. Suddenly, she wasn't so cold.

Nick, who appeared oblivious to her feelings, opened the door and turned on the light. "Shall we dine, milady." He motioned for her to enter the RV.

Unable to think of anything else, she responded with "please" and stepped into the camper. Immediately, she fell to the right and latched onto the table nearby.

"Problems?"

"No. I can manage." Not for the life of her would she admit anything was out of the ordinary. She studied the slope of the stove before asking Nick, who still had his feet planted firmly on the sloping ground, "How about a sandwich?"

"Gee, I had my heart set on a large platter of *hot* spaghetti and meatballs."

What she wouldn't give to have such a platter in hand to plop on his head. Maybe the red stringy spaghetti slipping and sliding over his rugged features would wipe that arrogant grin off his face. She began gathering the makings for sandwiches and something to put them on. She turned to hand him the ingredients only to discover he wasn't there, but a lantern glowed on the table.

Samantha managed after some effort, to get back outside with her arms full of food. She took one look at the table and cringed. They couldn't possibly put food on there. The glow from the lantern showed every grain of sand, tree and animal litter on the table. She looked at her arms full of goodies and then at Nick. He knelt before the fireplace, watching a small fire burn.

"Do we have a tablecloth?"

He swiveled to look up at her. From his expression, one would have thought she'd asked him to fly to the moon and bring her back a moon rock.

"This isn't your dining room table."

"I should hope not. This table is filthy. I won't be able to swallow a bite." She quivered at the thought.

He came to the table and brushed it with this hand. "There. That is the best I have to offer."

"But, the birds have…"

"A little sh…manure won't hurt you." He crossed his arms over his chest and grinned.

"You're enjoying this, aren't you?"

"Yep." He took the package of paper plates from her arms. Without ceremony, he plopped two plates on the table. "Just use the plates."

"Suppose the bread touches the litter?" She shuddered.

"Simple." He grabbed the bread. "You eat it anyway."

Her stomach flipped.

He motioned for her to put the food down. He proceeded to make himself a double-decker ham sandwich. Then he picked it up and took a large bite.

She knew the exact moment he spotted her staring at him. He stopped chewing and asked in a muffled voice, "What?"

"Aren't you going to serve me first?" A gentleman would have done so.

He stared at her and swallowed what he'd been eating before answering. "Serve you? This isn't a restaurant. It's called self-service." He nodded for her to begin.

Samantha swallowed hard. She would surely starve if she expected him to prepare the food. "Well, I've always—"

"Had a cook?"

"Yes." She stared at the fire knowing it would be far more sympathetic than the I-can't-believe-your-stupidity expression Nick must be wearing.

"You're kidding, right? Your mother never taught you how to cook?"

"Don't you fault my mother for skills she never needed."

"Excuuuuse me. I forgot the rich paid to have everything done for them." He bit into his sandwich and chewed.

"Of course." Samantha raised her head and stood proud. "Why should my mother, or I for that matter, learn to do such things when Sadie always prepared our food. She worked for my parents and stayed with me when I married Edward." She watched him eat, her mouth watering for a bite. It had been hours since lunch. "The kitchen was Sadie's domain."

"You hired her?"

"My mother did years ago.

"Then fire her."

"My goodness, no." What was he saying? "She's one of the family." Sadie might be a tyrant, but she was still family.

"Oh, hell. Here. Take mine." He held his sandwich out.

She stepped back. "But you've been eating it."

"So? You hungry or not?"

"Yes. But—"

"Then make your own damn sandwich." He stepped back, motioned toward the food, and plopped himself down on the table bench with all its debris.

"I will." She grabbed the bread and took great care

to place two slices on her plate without touching the table. She'd show him that she, at twenty-seven, could prepare a simple sandwich. Not much else, but she could do that one thing. Had done it many times before. She could also prepare her own cold cereal.

She finished preparing her food and looked for a place to sit. Not a clean spot to be had. "Yuck."

He wiped off a space on the bench for her. "Now sit down and eat."

And she did. No gourmet meal could have tasted better.

****

After they had eaten and repacked the food, Samantha sat at the table, staring into the fire. Nick poked at the coals a few times before sitting down next to her. The snapping of the fire prevented her from hearing anything in the woods but not from searching for glowing eyes in the dark. She felt safe with him sitting close. There was no doubt in her mind that he would protect her against any harm.

She also felt his nearness much more than she desired. Her insides were doing strange things, giving her feelings she'd never experienced before. Feelings she mustn't think about, not when she would be sleeping in such close proximity to him tonight. It was getting harder and harder to remember why she needed to keep her distance from this man. She racked her brain to think of something to say to distract her thoughts.

"This is nice. Very relaxing."

"Yeah. It is." He pulled on his ear. "I was thinking." He stared into the fire. "Maybe tomorrow we can find a better place and stay a day or two."

"I don't know much about camping." What an understatement. "The people around us seem to be enjoying living outside."

"Yeah." He leaned back to rest his elbows on the table, before stretching his long legs out in front of him. "I don't think we have much to worry about for a couple of days. It'll take that long for Vargas to get wind of our change in plans."

She'd forgotten the danger surrounding her. Had that letter she mailed to Vargas been a drastic mistake? She hoped not, but why did hindsight make her question her decision?

"Who'd guess we had killers on our tail?" Nick yawned.

Tell Nick about the letter.

She couldn't fathom how anyone could use that letter to find them while they were riding around the country in an RV. Who would believe it anyway? Her parents wouldn't. Why would Vargas? Yet, there could be some remote chance that it could be a trail to them.

Why didn't I think of this before?

He would be very angry when she told him about the letter and the cross. This would be a perfect time to discuss it, while he was calm and enjoying the evening. After several minutes of trying to think of a way to approach the subject, she decided she'd just say it. She turned toward him.

"I did something stupid." No answer. "I said—"

He snored. She swallowed her words. Relief spread through her. He's too tired to hear bad news tonight. She'd tell him first thing in the morning.

"Nick?" When he didn't respond to her voice she touched his shoulder. The next instant she was on her knees with her arm twisted behind her.

"Ouch! That hurts." She squirmed to get loose.

"Sam?" The moment he realized what he'd done, he released her and jumped away. "Did I hurt you?"

"You surprised me." He held out a hand to her, which she took. A jolt ran up her arm and into her stomach. Her gaze shot to his. Did her touch affect him in the same way?

"Don't ever put a hand on me when I'm sleeping."

That answered that question. Was that disappointment she felt? She bent over to brush the dirt from her knees to prevent him from reading the expression on her face.

"I didn't mean to frighten you," he said, his voice low.

"Do you always react this way at a simple touch?" A woman would have quite the problem sleeping with him. No touchy or take the chance of getting hurt. She wouldn't be in bed with this man, so she didn't have anything to worry about. What a shame. He might be as good in bed as he bragged that first night. He sure had the body to please this woman.

"Yeah." He moved away from her, staring into the blackness of the night. "Old habit. I should have warned you."

"You can rest assured I won't do it again."

"Smart woman." Nick rubbed his hands over his face. "Let's hit the sheets. I'm dead."

Samantha shuddered. "Please, don't say that word."

"Worried about me?" He wiggled his eyebrows.

"Under the circumstances, any sane person would be." He gave her one of his cocky, know-it-all grins.

Those butterflies fluttered in her stomach again. She tried to believe fear caused them but knew better.

****

Nick awoke as daylight began to creep around the curtains. After banging his elbows and head on hard paneling all night, he didn't get much sleep. Having a coffin-sized bunk over the cab of the RV didn't help either. At least her highness had the comfort of a nice queen size bed and the privacy of her own room. Though she was moving around right now, he'd heard her fall out of bed a couple times during the night. He grinned. He wasn't the only one having problems getting some shut-eye.

Later that afternoon, traveling west instead of east as previously planned, Nick took an unmarked dirt road back into a wooded area. Luck was with him. He'd found the perfect place for target practice—a small sand bank. Today, Samantha would learn how to handle and use his weapon.

Samantha looked around. "What on earth are we doing here? Where are the campgrounds?"

"Time for target practice."

"No. Oh. No." She shook her head and wrapped her arms around her backpack. "I'm not touching that piece of cold metal. You want to shoot it? Go right ahead."

"I don't need practice."

"Sure. You're probably a crack shot. Well, I want no part of even touching the thing, not to mention shooting it."

"Give me the piece." He held out his hand.

"I'm not handling the *piece*. It can rust apart before I'm picking it up."

"Then give me the backpack."

"No. It contains my personal things. Besides, gentlemen don't paw through a lady's purse." Her arms tightened around the bag.

"Hand it to me or I'll take it." He held out his hand. "Which will it be?" Her struggle to make a choice roused his curiosity. "What else are you hiding in there?"

"Just a few private women's things. Do you want to see my tampons?" She pretended to get one out to show him.

Nick shook his head. "Just give me the weapon." Damn the woman. She could sure turn things around on him fast.

"Okay. But I'm not using it." She reached in her bag and lifted the pistol out the same way she put it in—between her thumb and index finger.

Nick took it, checked the ammo. He got out of the RV and retrieved one of the targets he had purchased at the discount store the other day. He found a tree growing out of the bank about a man's height from the ground. He shot a couple rounds himself to check out everything for Samantha.

"Show off." Samantha stood behind him, seeing the two bullet holes in the center of the target and said, "I knew you didn't need practice."

"No. You do." He walked back to her. "Make up your mind to do this. You may need to know how to fire this weapon. It may mean the difference between you living or dying."

"I know I wouldn't be able to shoot anyone." She shook her head and walked away.

Nick waited, giving her time to digest his words.

Handling the Glock after seeing her husband shot and getting shot herself couldn't be easy. But she would learn how to use it.

Samantha stomped over to him, her back stiff as a post and her head high. "I don't want to, but I know I can do this. New experiences are good for me. They're all part of my new life."

"That a girl." Whatever excuse she wanted to use was okay by him. "All I want you to do is learn to use the weapon."

"Let's get to it."

His admiration for her climbed another notch. He marched her over to the place he had marked for her to stand. He wrapped her hand around the handle of the Glock 26. "No holding between your thumb and finger anymore."

"I know. I know." She gripped the gun, hands shaking.

"Try to steady yourself. Here, let me help you." Nick got behind her and wrapped his arms round her and his hands over hers on the weapon. Huge. Mistake. His heart started to race and another part of him woke up. The soft skin on her neck beckoned for his kiss. Inhaling her essence made him want to take her right there in the sand. Now, he was shaking. Yet, he knew no other way to help her aim and fire his weapon. He worked hard not to think about how perfectly she fit in his arms by locking his jaw and concentrating on the gun and the target.

****

Samantha's hold on the gun faltered. How was she ever going to do this when her body kept relaying signals to her mind that had nothing to do with the task at hand?

"I can't do this with you this close. Ah...I need room." She wiggled her backside, knowing she could work better without him wrapped around her.

Nick moaned in her ear. "Hold still. The gun might fire."

Realizing what she was doing to him, she stopped and didn't move another inch. Having him wrapped around her felt good. Really good.

"Just let me help you fire one shot."

"Okay. Just one." She couldn't take him rubbing against her any longer. She'd be lucky if she hit the top of the trees.

He gave her further instructions on the proper stance, aiming and squeezing the trigger. "There won't be much of a kickback, but be ready for one." She nodded. Took aim. Nick steadied her hands. "Pull," he ordered.

Easy for Mr. Expert to say, she thought, but she closed her eyes and did as directed. Her arms jumped from the force of the shot. The gun made a popping sound. A bird flew out of a nearby tree. The smell of gunpowder filled her nose. The bullet hit a root sticking out of the bank about five feet from the target.

"Not bad for the first time."

"At least I hit something, didn't I?" Hitting the sand happened to be more than she thought she would do.

He nodded. "Not bad. Let's try it again," he said, still wrapped around her.

"I want to do this on my own." She knew she could concentrate better without him making her hormones rise to dangerous levels.

Nick looked at her for a moment and stepped back. "You sure you can handle doing this on your own?"

Better than with him so darn close. "Yes. I can do anything, remember." Most of her shaking had been from his nearness or that's what she wanted to believe.

"Then let's do it."

With him coaching her all the way, Samantha got closer and closer to the target with each shot.

"That's enough for today."

"But I still haven't hit those circles." She motioned to the target. She couldn't blame her lack of accuracy on him this time. He hadn't touched her again except to level the weapon.

"You will."

"I wish I had your confidence." Doing anything with a gun put her miles out of her comfort zone.

"You're touching the weapon now. That's an improvement."

"I still don't like to. I do feel more comfortable being able to handle it the correct way."

"You'll get better." Nick motioned to the RV. "Put it back in your backpack." He picked up his target and headed for the RV.

He was right, but she could never shoot a man or any living thing. That she knew for a fact.

****

Nick pulled into a campsite outside of Amarillo. He'd headed west instead of east as previously planned, trying to put distance behind them. Anyone would be a fool to think he'd head back toward New York after what had happened thus far. His motto? "Lost in the "Big T".

Wearing his Stetson and dark glasses for

camouflage, he pulled up to the office door. They were miles from the campground they'd stayed at last night.

"Oh, this looks much better." A big smile brightened her face. "It paid to stop at that Information Center and make inquiries. We'd never have found this lovely secluded place. It's private and nice."

"Mmmmm." He wasn't about to admit she'd been right.

"Look. There's a lake. Mirror smooth, too. Beautiful."

Her happiness warmed his heart and put a grin on his face. Her eyes lit up and her beauty increased one hundred percent. His dumb heart was thudding hard in his chest.

"This is new to me. I can't wait to get my toes in the water. It looks crystal clear."

"I'd think you'd prefer a nice clean chlorinated pool."

"I've been in the ocean, and that isn't clean or chlorinated."

Her chin shot up like it always did when she was being indignant. The light in her eyes faded too, which made him feel worse than the crap a duck had left on the ground near his feet. His making statements about her status in life wouldn't do much to keep her safe. Why did he say such things? Not to hurt her, that's for sure. Liking her too much might be the problem, though he worked hard not to let his emotions get the better of him where she was concerned.

Nick tipped his head. "I stand corrected." He hated to bust her bubble, but he added, "Don't forget why we're here. Forget that and trouble will sneak up from behind."

"You worry too much. Who's going to find us out here anyway?" Suddenly, she covered her mouth and looked away.

"What?"

"Nothing."

What had she done? "Then why did you turn a pasty white?"

"I-I just…It's nothing, really."

"Is there something I should know?"

Before she could answer, a man stepped up to the car. "Can I help you, sir?"

He heard a sigh of relief from Samantha. She was hiding something. He knew trouble would be attached to whatever she was keeping secret.

In less than an hour, he had the RV parked and ready for use. What a difference level ground made. Either that or he was beginning to get the hang of this camping stuff. Maybe it would be more fun than he imagined.

Samantha's giggle brightened Nick's mood. She acted like a child who'd found a new playhouse. She explored the entire site being careful not to touch anything or to dirty her hands. She hadn't fooled him with her actions with the flashlight last night. He'd heard those twigs snapping, too.

"Isn't this wonderful? We were lucky to get a campsite on the water. Do you think we could go wading?"

"Sure. Be my guest."

"Not now, silly." A big grin brightened her face. "After we finish setting up camp. Goodness! I never dreamed I'd ever be saying those words." She laughed. "Setting up camp," she repeated. "Isn't it terrific?"

"Oh, yeah." Since he'd just done all the work. He rubbed the back of his neck. Maybe, for the first time in her life, Samantha Chadwick-Thorne was acting like a little girl. She made him feel good deep inside. Her cheerfulness was infectious. To his surprise, he found himself whistling while he opened the awning and set the poles. Samantha surprised him by setting up the two new lawn chairs they had purchased earlier. That's the first "work" she'd done. He pulled the picnic table under the awning. She placed the new bright red and white-checkered plastic tablecloth on it. The minute she spotted it in the store, she grabbed the package and tossed it in the cart.

"Look, Cindy Lou's apron. We've got to have one of these. What would your Cindy Lou say if she saw you wrapped in one of these, *Stud*?" She had giggled at his glare, but she amused him.

She had been driving him crazy for four days. She added to his problem by the way she stretched to cover the corners of the table. Her cute little bottom wiggled right under his nose, setting him on fire. She hadn't a clue to the effect she had on a man, especially, a sexually deprived man such as himself. It was a good thing he had iron control, or he'd throw her on that checkered cloth and teach her why he deserved to be called "stud".

The sudden coming awake of his anatomy made him curse. Time to move her out of his reach. He headed down to the water. Maybe he needed a swim in the cold pond to cool off. Parts of him were burning red hot.

"I just love this place," Samantha said a few minutes later, standing next to him. "Oh, look!" She grabbed his arm and pointed out into the lake. "A mama duck and her babies. They're coming this way."

Nick couldn't speak with her breast resting on his arm. A bolt of lightning made a direct hit on his groin. What a hell of a surprise she would get if she didn't move it soon. And with those baby ducks watching, too.

"I'm going to get some bread." She released his arm and hurried away.

His breath hissed through his teeth. "You do that," he mumbled, his arm still burning from her touch.

The mama duck and her babies touched the shore and waddled after her. Nick could do no less. When she came back outside with bread in hand, the little family teetered back and forth on their webbed feet and quacked for all they were worth.

"You're such cute little things. Are you hungry?" She broke open the loaf of bread and began feeding the ducks, squealing in delight as they snapped a piece from her hand. One baby pushed another aside with its flapping wings.

"Don't be a little piggy. Brothers share with sisters."

"How do you know which is which?" Nick grinned, enjoying this properly trained, sophisticated lady acting like a child.

"He's so aggressive. He has to be a guy."

"Oh? And women aren't?"

"No. My mother claims women are the gentle sex." She broke off another chunk and handed it to the mama duck.

Nick snorted. "Those words would insult some women."

"No doubt, in your line of work." She fed yet

another duck, and it nibbled at her finger. She laughed. "Now be careful little one. We don't bite the hand feeding us."

"Good point. Speaking of food, I'm starved." For her. The urge to taste her grew with each breath. Man, he was in severe lust.

He cleared his throat. "Are we eating before those creatures gobble up all our fixings?

"Humph! Self-service, remember?" With that she whispered sweet goodbyes to the ducks and flounced back to the RV.

Mama duck must have sided with Samantha because she gathered her family and waddled back to the lake. Their squawking could be heard all the way back to the water. He now knew what it felt like to be snubbed by a beautiful woman and a flock of damned ducks.

Hell. He was in deep trouble with this woman.

Chapter 8

Nick stepped out of the RV into the frigid morning air. What he wouldn't give for a heavy coat. These old jeans and black and white plaid flannel shirt didn't do the trick. He should have grabbed his sweatshirt, too. On the other hand, shivering was good. It helped to rid his mind of the visions he had of Samantha sleeping in the flimsy nightgown he'd picked out for her at the discount store. Not to mention the one of her wearing nothing at all. Parts of him remained attentive regardless.

No way in hell did he want to become involved with her. They were physically too close in that tin box. His chest was still red hot from where she had rubbed against him on her way to the bedroom last night. He had no doubt the incident had sparked the burning fire in him during the night, causing him to wake with the kind of dream he hadn't had since he was thirteen. Build a fire. That should take his mind off Sam and keep him warm, too.

Once the flames blazed and sparks flew into the morning air, he plopped in a lawn chair in front of the fire to watch it burn. The sudden sound of gravel crunching under someone's shoes brought him to full alert. Everything in him tensed. He put his hand near his gun. Carelessness could get them both killed. He eased out of his chair and turned to face his visitor.

Overwhelming relief weakened him. His knees would've buckled if he hadn't locked them. A young dark-haired boy leaned against a tree in front of their campsite.

"Hi," Nick offered.

"Hi." The boy stuck his hands in the pockets of his ragged cut offs. He looked everywhere but at Nick.

"Out kind of early aren't ya?"

He shrugged.

"Little chilly this morning."

Another shrug of his shoulders.

"You camped near here?" He'd have to speak to answer that question, Nick thought.

He pointed down the road.

Guess not. "Your parents still sleeping?"

Up went his shoulders one more time. He'd said "hi" proving he could talk. Must be shy. "Want to join me by the fire? The heat feels real good." Nick held both hands up to the flames.

This time he took a step forward. Encouraged, Nick set up the other lawn chair next to him. "Come on, son. Have a seat." He hesitated and took a step backward this time. Cautious. Nice going, kid. By the looks of him, he couldn't be more than seven or eight. His once white T-shirt had turned a dingy gray, and he wore no jacket. The temperature had dropped overnight. He had to be cold.

"Suit yourself." Nick exaggerated a shiver and began buttoning his shirt. "I plan on taking in some of this heat." He moved his chair closer to the fire and sat down. He offered nothing more. It took a few moments before footsteps crunched on the gravel. Nick stared into the fire. Soon, his company moved the chair a few feet away and sat down. He couldn't be getting much warmth from that angle. Past experience had taught him to ease off and let kids make their own moves. He waited for him to speak.

"Nice RV."

"Yeah, it is." Nick broke another long silence with, "Where's your mama?"

"Sleepin'." He hugged himself.

"Your dad?" Nick glanced at him, needing to see his expression.

He dug his toe back and forth in the dirt several times before saying, "Don't have one."

"Sorry." He had heard that statement many times before from kids whose fathers were dead or didn't want them. The desertion hurts. Bad. He knew the feeling well. There was a time he wanted his father too, but no longer. "Won't she be worried if you're gone when she wakes up?"

"She knows I'm around."

He didn't like the sound of that. His guess would be that this little cub was on his own most of the time. Somebody should be keeping an eye on him. After all, he could be a child molester instead of a cop.

"You got kids?"

"Nope." Nick wasn't surprised at the question. Every kid he ever worked with wanted to know if he had children. It tugged hard on his heart. He had seen many lonely boys, but somehow this one got to him. Fast. Maybe it was the torn clothing, the holes in his sneakers or the lack of a dad. Or maybe it was that sad look in his eyes. Maybe all of it, but he liked him right away.

The kid moved his chair a few inches closer to the

fire but said nothing more. Nick picked up the slack. "I'm Nick." He offered him the high-five sign so popular with the boys he worked with at the Neighborhood Home for Boys. The lad stared at his palm, then at Nick. He kept his gaze locked with the boy's. This young man needed to know he was treating him as an equal.

"Joey," he said and slapped palms with Nick.

"Nice to meet you, Joey." Joey nodded and jammed his hand in his pocket. "Camp much?"

"Yeah." Joey watched the flames.

"You and your mom on a vacation?"

"Nope."

Nick stared into the fire, not liking the thought swishing in his head. "You always lived around here?"

"Naw. We camp lots of places."

Yep. He'd been right. A succession of campgrounds was Joey's home. Damn. He'd seen too many kids without homes. He pulled a Tootsie Roll from his pocket. "Want one?" Joey shook his head but kept his gaze on the candy. Nick unwrapped it and popped it in his mouth. "I love these things. Have some on me all the time." He chewed for a moment, then added, "One of the guys I play ball with back home got me hooked on these things."

"You play ball?" Joey's eyes brightened.

"Sometimes." Nick pulled out another piece of candy and offered it to him. This time, Joey didn't hesitate. In seconds, he had it jammed in his mouth. The kid acted starved to death.

"Wanna play sometime?" Joey asked in a muffled mouth-full-of-candy sort of way.

He smiled. "You got a ball?"

Joey grinned. "A bat and glove too."

"You're on."

****

Samantha stood by the open window and listened to the interaction between Nick and the child. Interesting how the mention of a ball and a piece of candy could attract men of all ages. She had been sound asleep when the sound of voices awoke her. Remembering other voices in the night gave her a brief scare. There would be times, like now, when the memory of Edward's death would come back with an overwhelming force. But she wouldn't let it take over her life. She searched for something else to think about.

Burgundy, pink, beige or a combination thereof covered everything in the RV—drapes, bedspread, floor, and walls. It looked great but very boring. She laughed every time she entered the pint-sized bathroom. It would fit into a small corner of the one in her home. The kitchen area had everything she would need if she knew how to cook. Samantha opened the miniature refrigerator and grabbed a bottle of orange juice.

The few belongings she had purchased at the discount store hung in one of the closets located on each side of the queen-sized bed. She didn't feel guilty sleeping in such comfort while Nick slept in the bunk over the cab. He had insisted on sleeping up there.

She never dreamed RV's could be this comfortable. Maybe she could learn to like this camping thing. Her mother, on the other hand, would faint dead away if she could see a Chadwick "roughing" it.

Mother would go insane at the thought of her society daughter living in such close quarters with a man other than her husband. A man she had been having erotic sex with all night—in her dreams. She wondered if the actual act would live up to the fantasy. Should she attack him to find out?

Four years of sex with Edward had never been as exciting as one night in dreamland with her bodyguard. She'd do better to remember Nick, being a cop, liked the excitement and risk involved in the job. She didn't want to live a life with a man who was in constant danger. She rested her forehead against the cool window to breathe in the crisp air. Why was she thinking about him in that way? A way that could never happen. His attitude about her financial status would put an end to anything that might get started between them. What had a woman done to him to make him feel the way he did? A movement outside caught her attention. Joey. She loved children.

Joey returned, carrying his bat and glove. Watching the child and Nick made her smile. With those dark eyes and dark hair, the boy would someday be a charmer. She frowned. How could a mother leave her young child alone in a public campground? While she slept? Worked? Weren't there rules against such things?

Samantha's own life had been controlled, but there never had been a day when she didn't feel protected. Did Joey have a similar safety net around him? She'd guess not. She made a mental note to do something about his situation when she got back home. First, she wanted to meet this young man. She slipped into her new jeans and bypassed the sexy green thing for a sapphire, long sleeved T-shirt and headed for the door.

"Nick? I thought I heard voices." Samantha came

out of the RV pulling on a sweater and headed toward him. "Oh! A visitor." She held out her hand. "My name is Sa—"

"Sara, meet Joey." He took her hand, pulling her near to wrap his arm around her waist.

She stared up at him. He arched his eyebrow. She could feel a blush creep into her face. If it weren't for him she'd have blurted out her own name—again. She sighed. She just wasn't very good at role-playing. Or hiding from a murderer. She didn't care if he was pretending or not. His warm strong arms felt great wrapped around her. Nick drew her closer. Warmth flowed through her despite the cool air.

"Joey, this is my wife, Sara."

Joey had his ball and glove stuck under his arm while both of his hands were rammed in his pockets. The toe of one holey sneaker dug in the dirt. Samantha looked at Nick and caught the slight shake of his head, his signal not to offer her hand.

"Pleased to meet you, Joey."

Still digging a ditch with his foot, Joey mumbled, "Kay."

"Wanna go an inning or two with us, Sara?"

Joey's mouth fell open almost as wide as she imagined hers had done. Samantha Chadwick-Thorne play ball? Nick must have forgotten she had been politely ordered by all the coaches at school to please not participate in sports.

"I think I'll...ah...pass this time." Was that a sign of relief she heard from Joey? Nick was so close she could feel him chuckle rather than hear him. He did remember. She elbowed him. His "oomph" pleased her. "Maybe next time."

While Nick and Joey played catch on the road by the campsite, Samantha went back into the RV to check her backpack, something she did several times a day. She unzipped her bag, ignored the gun, and gave a sigh of relief when she spotted her grandmother's jewels nestled in the bag along with the two jars of cleanser and moisturizer.

When would she get the nerve to tell Nick about the cross and the letter to Vargas? He already thought she was part of Edward's murder.

Chapter 9

Pacing the campsite at the crack of dawn seemed to be Nick's daily routine of late. Not to mention freezing his butt off. Man. His shivers had shivers. Today happened to be a traveling day or he'd build a roaring fire.

A man's muscles could get real soft camping day after day. Yesterday, he'd gotten more exercise playing ball with Joey than he'd gotten in days. He'd need all his strength when he met up with Vargas. He dropped to the ground and did fifty pushups.

Last night had been great. He and Samantha had sat in silence in front of the fire and chilled. He'd felt more relaxed than he had in a long time. What would the captain or his wife, Mary, have thought had they seen him this comfortable with a woman again?

The captain! Holy Hell. He hadn't called him in several days. The man would be giving him a verbal lashing that could be heard in Paris. "Call me daily." That's what the man had ordered. Nick ran his fingers through his hair. He was in deep trouble. They needed to get on the road. He headed to the RV to wake Samantha. He opened the door to find her dressed in jeans and a light blue T-shirt that left nothing for him to imagine. And his imagination had already been working overtime where she was concerned. She reached for her navy sweatshirt and everything on her moved. The hole he was falling into got deeper and deeper. All he could do was stare.

"We're traveling today, aren't we?"

He shook his head and gave himself a loud mental lecture on how a bodyguard and a witness didn't mix. "Let's hit the road," he grumbled.

"What about breakfast? I can—"

"Later. You've got some target shooting to do this morning." He knew his tone was sharp, but he couldn't stand there another second and look at her. Nick closed the door and turned to get the RV ready to roll.

In a shaking voice, Joey said, "You leavin'?"

Startled, Nick crouched and turned with his hand on his weapon. Joey. Damn. He eased his hand off his piece. If he didn't keep his mind off Samantha and back on the job, he'd get them both killed.

"Jeesh, you scared me, Joey." He stopped to look at the young man. The kid had no jacket and was shivering. He looked like he would cry at any minute. "We have to move on."

"Where you g-gonna go?"

"Here. There. No special place."

"Oh."

The disappointment in the kid's eyes broke his heart. "I bet I have a minute to toss a few. You game?" He had yet to meet Joey's mother. Did she realize how lonely and desperate the kid was for a father? Did she care?

"I g-got a minute." He took off on a run.

"Okay! You're on," Nick yelled. Maybe exercise would warm the kid.

While Joey ran to get his ball, Nick whipped his sweatshirt over his head and tossed it on the ground.

"Kids shouldn't have to be brought up this way," he mumbled, his breath steaming in the cool morning air.

****

Samantha, having readied everything inside for traveling, stepped outside to watch the guys. Nick taking the time to play one more time with the boy tickled a spot around her heart. He really was a good man. He, a macho cop, had a heart filled with compassion and love for children.

"Put your weight into it, Joey," Nick instructed. Joey pulled back and threw another one. "Perfect."

Joey's pleased expression brightened the day and warmed her all over. An idea started to form in her head. There were a lot of children, like Joey, who needed a helping hand. Her mind reeled with ideas. She could work with underprivileged children or organize her own foundation to help them. Either way, she made a promise to herself that she would do something for Joey. First, she had to put Chico Vargas in jail forever.

"Nice game, kiddo." Nick rubbed the boy's head.

A huge grin spread across Joey's face. "Thanks."

"You know, all this time and I don't know your last name."

"Mitchell."

"Joey Mitchell. I won't forget it." Nick held up his hand to exchange a high five. "Maybe we'll see you again."

"You comin' back?" Joey's eyes lit up.

"Probably not right away."

The light vanished. Joey looked down at his feet, moving the dirt around with his foot once again. "We're movin', too."

"Then we'll see you when we do, partner."

Samantha had to force a smile. She hadn't realized until that moment the poor child lived in a tent *year-round*. She was more determined than ever to see that Joey had a better chance at life.

Nick pull out his notebook and wrote something in it before he tore a page out and handed it to Joey. "I won't be home for a few days, but call collect. I'd be happy to hear from you."

Joey took the paper and studied the number. He turned his back to Nick and wiped his face on his short sleeve. When he had himself composed, he turned back. "Thanks, but I ain't callin'."

"That's okay. Keep the number anyway." He reached for Samantha's hand. "Ready, Sweetheart?"

She didn't move for a moment. His endearment rang in her ears. It sounded natural flowing from his lips.

"Bye, Mrs. Sara."

The use of her cover name jarred her back to reality. Nick was studying her with his eyebrows arched and his hand held out for her to take. She took his hand and immediately found herself close to him with his arm wrapped around her waist. His touch felt so good.

"Ah...Good bye, Joey. Maybe we'll meet again soon." Samantha would make sure she did.

"Let's head 'em up. Move 'em out." Nick roared like an old wagon master. Joey grinned, but it didn't quite reach his sad eyes.

Samantha's heart did a flip-flop at his attempt to lighten things for the child. She watched Joey through the side mirror and didn't miss his downcast head and the continual digging in the dirt with his shoe. He'd lost a good friend in Nick. The heartbreaking expression on

Nick's face proved the feeling was mutual.

Suddenly, Joey was yelling and waving something in the air. "Stop. You forgot your sweatshirt."

"No. I didn't."

Samantha smiled and patted his arm. "You're a nice guy."

"No, I'm not."

She saw the muscles in his throat tighten as he fought for control. Yes, he was. His tough guy act no longer fooled her.

****

They stopped for breakfast around 9 a.m. at a truck stop south of Amarillo. After eating, Nick found a public phone, punched in the captain's number, and waited for the connection. Busy. He hung up and waited. He watched Samantha roam the gift shop, but his mind kept picturing Joey's gloomy expression as they drove away.

He scratched his chest. He'd only known Joey a couple days, but the kid had gotten to him. Why did kids have to put up with such crap? It made him angry. Why couldn't Joey's mother afford an apartment instead of a tent? Why wasn't his father there to care for him? Why hadn't Nick's own father been there for him? Why had his mother worked herself to death while his father conned everyone and everything in his path? He didn't know where his Dad was and could care less. He pulled on his ear. The less he thought about his old man, the better for both of them. He dialed the captain again.

"Captain Bianco."

"Hey. Where you been?"

"It's about damn time. Why the hell haven't you

been in touch?" the captain yelled.

Nick pulled the phone away from his ear for a second. "Whooooa, Captain. I've been doing my job as you ordered."

"Your *job* included calling me every day."

Nick was sure the veins were bulging on the guy's neck. "I've been a little busy."

"No phones where you are, Detective?"

"Not always." Judging by the silence that followed, Nick had surprised his boss. "I didn't mean to worry you." Nick felt the fingers of guilt crawl into his head. Sam had him tied in knots, but his boss wouldn't appreciate hearing him say so.

"How's the lady?"

"She's anxious to testify."

"I bet she is." Bianco was silent for a moment. "What's going on, Detective?"

"What do you mean?" Did the man have mental telepathy?

"I've gotten calls from the motels you were supposed to stay at for the last three nights informing me that you hadn't shown up. The Department still got charged."

"Hell, Captain, I forgot about the reservations." Nick pulled on his ear. "Vargas' goons almost got to your star witness. I figured someone got our schedule from the computer. Do you think Vargas could have a hacker on his payroll?"

Silence. Then, "Anything's possible where that low-life is concerned."

"Do you think the phone is safe?" Nick always used a pay phone to prevent his calls from being traced.

"Just a minute."

By the sounds he heard, Nick knew the captain was checking his phone.

"Clear on this end."

"Good." Nick ran his fingers through his hair. "Since Samantha's attempted kidnapping—"

"What kidnapping?"

"That's right. You didn't know." He proceeded to tell his boss what happened at their last motel. "We decided to switch to Plan B."

"Plan B? Did we have one?"

He switched the phone to the other ear. Samantha headed toward him. "We're camping."

"Camping? In a tent?"

"No. We rented an RV." Nick still couldn't believe it and understood the captain's surprise. A long silence followed.

"I don't believe it. You? Her? Camping?"

"Yeah. How about that?" He smiled to himself, knowing the captain was in shock. Then he explained why and how they decided on the RV.

"But…You've never camped a day in your life, son."

"I have now. Kind of like it too." Those intimate rubs in close quarters against a certain female sure did make it fun. Samantha stood about ten feet away waiting for him.

"Wait a minute. Where did you get the money? You didn't charge—"

"The lady is rich, my friend, and she carries a lot of dough with her." She must have picked it up at her house. He wasn't about to tell the captain they had made a detour. "It's a long story, but so far it's worked out."

"You're confined in a small area. You'd be sitting ducks. You sure about this?"

He sure knew about that small area thing. Hell. He liked to rub against and do other unmentionables to a beautiful sexy woman. What man wouldn't? "It's a good cover, Captain. No one knows where we are except you."

"The less people who know, the better."

"Exactly." He didn't even want his boss to know for fear someone would be listening.

"What's your location?"

He refused to give an exact location. "South of Amarillo."

"Texas?" The captain's voice raised an octave. "I thought you would be heading back east for the trial."

"That's what Vargas would expect."

"Thus Plan B? I get it. Smart move, Detective."

Nick smiled. "You know me well, friend."

"Yes. I do. You're going to make it back here for the trial, aren't you, Detective?"

"Wouldn't miss it." He decided this was a good chance to ask the question that has plagued him since he left Albany. "How's Mike doing? Is he working on the Thorne murder?"

"Mike? No. Why?"

"Just wondered. I know he wanted the case."

"Bauer is temporarily working your case load with him."

"Bauer's good." If Mike wasn't working the Thorne homicide, why had he been at Samantha's house the day they left? Nick still couldn't come up with a valid reason for Mike to be there unless he was working with Vargas. Mike had been in on their plans.

Man, he didn't want to believe it. He ran his fingers through his hair. This didn't look good.

"Not as good as you." Silence once again filled the line before the captain began to chuckle. "Two city slickers camping." Bianco laughed out loud this time. "The more I think about it, the better I like it. Got to hand it to you. It's a clever cover. I knew you were the man for this job."

Nick's cheeks warmed. Compliments embarrassed him. It reminded him of the number of times he longed for his own father to tell him he done something well. He never had.

"Listen. I've got to get going." He glanced toward Samantha. She stood staring into space. Worrying, no doubt.

"Okay. Be sure to call me tomorrow."

"Sure thing." If I can, he thought.

"That's an order, Detective."

"Yes, sir." Order or not, it depended on his situation.

"Take care."

"Always, Captain." Which was a lie of late. Lust for a particular gorgeous woman kept getting in the way. It had to stop today.

He hung up the receiver. Once more he thought about Mike, and he didn't like what he was thinking. Maybe he'd call Amy Bauer. He flipped through his book for her extension.

"Are you calling Mike?"

"No. Detective Bauer." It took seconds to dial her number. Her voice mail picked up. He disconnected the call. Investigating his partner wasn't something he wanted recorded.

****

They arrived in the outskirts of Lubbock later that afternoon and stopped for a late lunch. It started to rain, making Samantha frown. Nick's mood had become as dark as the weather. Something the captain had said must have alerted him to an emergency. He had insisted on her target shooting in some secluded place he'd found. She'd at least hit the target today. She didn't want to admit this, but the gun did feel more comfortable in her hand.

They had made good time. They were in Midland by dinnertime. According to the brochure she'd picked up at the gas station, Midland was one of the oil centers of the state. She glanced out of the window. Oil rigs were everywhere.

"I wonder if any of those wells belong to George W?"

"Huh? What?"

"Nothing. Just making conversation." She hated short answers, but something was bothering him again.

"Mmmmm."

Not long after that brief exchange, Nick pulled into a small private campground. They had decided to stay away from the larger well-known state-owned places in favor of the secluded less populated private ones.

"We need to get milk."

"Okay." He eased into a parking space at the camp store. "See if they have any Tootsie Rolls."

She couldn't believe his words. "You aren't coming in?"

"Naw." He motioned with his hand for her to go. "Make it fast."

He always shopped or was within sight of her.

Now, he really did have her worried. She did her shopping in record time and rushed back to the RV. With the steady downpour, it didn't take them long to settle on their campsite for the night. His mood seemed to improve once he had the electricity and water plugged in and the heater working.

Tonight was Samantha's turn to cook. They would feast on potato chips, toasted cheese sandwiches and tomato soup prepared under his supervision. One of the first things she vowed to do after testifying was to take cooking classes. She never wanted to be caught feeling incompetent again.

Nick removed his gun and holster and placed it on the counter before opening the refrigerator door. "Want a soda?"

"Please."

He brought out a lemon mist and a coke along with the butter and cheese. He popped the tops on the soda and placed the lemon one next to her on the counter.

Samantha reached down in the bottom cupboard for a pan. In such close quarters, her backside collided with his, causing her to bounce forward. Before Nick could reach her, she caught herself on the cabinet door.

"You okay?"

"Yes." No! He'd just scorched her derriere. How in the world could she be okay?

"I didn't mean—"

"I know. It's very cramped in here." She busied her hands retrieving the pan in an effort not to rub the burning spot on her fanny.

Nick appeared to be unaffected by what happened. She, on the other hand, found it difficult to take a normal breath. Maybe concentrating on dinner would help.

She opened the upper cupboard to get the bread. Nick stepped up behind her. "Here, shorty. Let me get that for you." He leaned against her entire backside placing his left hand on her shoulder.

Her eyelids fluttered shut. The faint smell of lime aftershave filled her senses. Her every thought centered on the heat generating from him and the pleasant tingling sensation wherever his body touched hers. Never in her life had she felt such sensations, such desire from a man's touch. She froze in place, not daring to move. When he stepped back, she grabbed her soda and took a long drink in an effort to cool her rising temperature.

"You didn't do half bad hitting the target today."

"Better than the first time, but still not good." Yes, let's change the topic.

"You'll get better. Give yourself time."

"I don't have a year to learn." Not that she wanted to.

"Each day you'll be better than the day before." He took a long swallow of his soda.

"I'm glad you've got confidence in me. It's something I lack." She took a sip of hers, too.

He took a couple cans of tomato soup from another cupboard and set them on the counter near Samantha. Her stomach fluttered. Goodness, how would she ever make it through the evening trapped by the weather in this small area?

"Samantha?"

"Be patient. I'm cooking as fast as I can."

"You've got to open the can before you pour the soup into the pan." He snickered.

"I know that."

He nodded toward the pan. Yee gads. She was shaking the sealed can over the pan. "I was just getting the feel of how to empty the can."

"Sure, you were." A know-it-all grin pulled at his mouth. "Here. Try this. It's easier to get the soup out with this." He held what looked like a two-legged miniature tripod.

"Give me the darn thing." She yanked it out of his hand.

He knew. Blast the man. He knew the effect he had on her. Why must he study her with such a concentrated sexy gaze?

"Gosh, it's warm in here." She fanned herself. Samantha tried her darnedest to make the contraption fit on the can, but to no avail. He took pity on her and took it from her shaking hand. Just in time or she would have whipped it at him to wipe that stupid grin off his face. Looking at him was impossible. He couldn't miss how scorching hot he made her feel. Darn.

She was melting faster than the butter she picked up, and then dropped, back on the counter. She wanted him to hold her as a man should hold a woman. *Stop being a fool.* She directed her gaze to the can of soup and waited for the demonstration. He wrapped his muscular arms around her. She caught her breath. He placed the knife-like edge on the can and squeezed the two pencil-like legs together. Unable to take her gaze from the muscles working in his arms, she suddenly felt faint.

"You can breathe any time now," Nick whispered.

Samantha took a deep breath. The lid clicked on the final turn. He gave her a quick squeeze. *Oh.*

Gracious. She didn't know a man's touch could be this potent.

"Think you can do the other can?"

His words snapped her back to the here and now. "Of course"—she cleared her throat—"but only if you back off and stand over there." She pointed to the opposite end of the small room. His loud hoarse laugh filled the RV, but he dropped his arms. At last she could breathe. Instead of doing as instructed, he leaned his hips against the counter only inches away.

It wasn't as far away as she wanted him to be, but it would do. He gave her directions on preparing the soup and grilling the sandwiches. Samantha willed her fingers not to shake and her legs to hold her upright. Part of her mind concentrated on what he told her to do. The other part urged her to stop and ravish him.

His nearness alone overheated her entire system. Her nipples were sensitive, craving his touch. A very female part of her sent out fulfillment needs to her brain. He did more, just being Nick, to make her desire him than any man had before. That included Edward. Oh, my. What was she doing to herself? This was not appropriate now, or ever. This man was her bodyguard. But oh, how she wanted him to play guard over her naked body.

Nick's intensive gaze creased his forehead. He'd read her thoughts. Samantha couldn't stop the blush that crept up her neck and into her face. Darn the man!

I'm a lady. I'd better start acting like one.

Chapter 10

Beautiful. Captivating. Sexy. Arousing.

Yet, mega words to describe Samantha. She sipped her soda. Nick watched the delicate movement of her throat. Even that echoed of class. He rammed his hands in his pockets to keep from grabbing her like some Neanderthal.

Remembering he'd had his fill of rich women and feeling less than worthy didn't matter a damn bit. Even his job to protect her didn't put a crack in his desire for her. What else could a man do but watch this seductive creature biting her lip and concentrating so hard on trying to accomplish something she'd never done? The effort she put into doing her part only increased his admiration for her.

Face it, chump, you really like her.

He frowned. Yeah, he did. But that's as far as he'd go. Nick's thoughts were interrupted when he realized what she was doing. "Hey, watch the butter."

"What's it doing?" She leaned closer to look.

He grinned, pointing to the bread. "You trying to clog my arteries?"

"Oh. I didn't realize." With her lower lip between her teeth and using a table knife, Samantha scraped off the excess butter.

"It helps if you keep your mind on the job."

"It'd help if you moved far away from me." Her

face got very red.

"Me? I'm just supervising." He crossed his arms, then his feet and chuckled to himself.

"You're the problem. You make me forget my own name."

"Is that so?" He couldn't stop the cheeky grin spreading across his face. And she saw it, too.

"Oh. No." She covered her mouth with her hands. "I take it back. Forget I said that."

"Not on your life. It's the nicest thing you've passed my way since we've been on this joy ride." He liked picking on her. She made some of the cutest faces.

"You're a tease." She waved him off and got back to her scraping.

He laughed out loud. "You're something else, Sam."

"Thank you. I'll take that as a compliment."

Her smile was quick and bright. It made a direct hit in his groin. His groan may have been silent, but it rocked him like an earsplitting explosion. This woman was driving him crazy with a capital "C." Colliding with various body parts in this small space was one thing. Then he'd done that fool thing of wrapping his arms around her to demonstrate the use of the can opener. He'd done it to get a reaction, but it backfired.

Real dumb, O'Reilly.

Nick hadn't missed the interested glances she'd tossed his way lately. He could read her like a well-lighted billboard in the dead of night. He needed to cool off. He moved to do so, until she looked up at him. He turned into one sick puppy. Every thought he had centered on the hot desire he saw in her eyes. His heart did a flip-flop in his chest. His damn breath flew out the door which is where he should be headed right now.

"What are you doing?" She gasped when Nick reached in front of her and turned off the burners.

"This." He turned her around and wrapped his arms around her. Her weak, "Oh" made him hesitate. "I'm going to kiss you, Sam. If you don't want me to, speak up now."

The way she studied him, he thought she would tell him where to go and the fastest means of transportation. To his amazement, she stood on her toes, locked her hands behind his neck and gave him a wide-open, tongue groping wet kiss. Not only couldn't he think, but she also propelled all his good intentions out the door along with his earlier loss of breath.

She tasted of lemon and smelled like vanilla ice cream, his favorite. She moaned. He groaned in return. Falling against her in the safe house had been his downfall. For five days, he'd been in a living hell fighting his desire for her. Today, the battle ended. Samantha had won.

Nick nibbled at her soft neck with tender lip bites. His imagination hadn't done justice to the texture of her skin. Not like Scotch, smooth and smoky, as he'd thought, but smooth and fragrant as a rose petal. The starving need to taste her had him raising his head to feed his hunger again.

Still locked together, Nick leaned against the counter to cradle her between his legs. Indescribable pleasure ripped through him, tearing a moan from his throat. Samantha's little gasps and wiggles set off a volcanic eruption in him unlike any he had experienced in his thirty-four years.

His fiery need for her became more intense than

any red-hot lava flow, and just as destructive to all the little voices in his head telling him to run while he still could. He fought hard for control—a battle he was on a fast track to losing with the small circling motions Samantha kept making with her hips against a very needy part of him. He had to have her now.

He eased back and looked into her deep green dazed eyes. What he saw rocked him so hard, it almost knocked him off his feet. He swooped her up in his arms and headed straight for her bedroom with one image in his head—Samantha naked. He whacked his elbow on the narrow doorframe so hard his whole arm tingled. Nothing deterred him from this mission. He laid her on the bed with him on top of her.

"Yes," Samantha whispered, clinging to his neck.

He found her luscious lips once again, feasting on them like a hungry bear coming out of hibernation. He managed to release the buttons on her blouse without breaking their kiss. He just couldn't get enough of her and needed to touch her everywhere. She touched his stomach trying to release the snap on his jeans. That fumbling sent a message to his feeble brain.

When did sex become part of the job, old man?

Nick yanked back, pulling her arms away from him and rolled over on the bed. He covered his eyes with his hands. What the hell was he doing? This wasn't part of the job. All it could do was interfere with his mind and get them both killed. "Sorry, Sam."

"What happened? Did I do something wrong?" She pulled her blouse together.

"You did everything right. It's me."

Confused, she stared at him. "I thought…"

He turned to her and looked her in the eyes. "I'm a

cop, your bodyguard. I'm—"

A sudden tap on the outside door brought Nick to his feet. Then came more persistent knocking.

His gaze shot to Samantha. "Someone's at the door," he whispered. "Get dressed and keep out of sight." He locked the bedroom door behind him.

Nick eased into the kitchen and retrieved his weapon from the counter, cursing himself for not having it on his person. Vargas' goons could have shot their way in, then they both would be dead. "Dammit to hell and back. Some bodyguard I turned out to be," he mumbled.

Their caller pounded on the door. "Hey. Anyone in there?"

"Just a minute," Nick yelled. He slid his finger in back of the curtain to check outside and saw the kid from the office. He gave a sigh of relief. He tucked his gun in the back of his pants and unlocked the door, keeping the screen between them. If the kid tried anything, Nick could send him flying by pushing the screen in his face.

"Is something wrong?"

"I hope I didn't interrupt anythin'." The kid was doing his best to peer around Nick at the inside of the RV.

"Not a thing." *Everything.* The kid just stopped him from making a complete fool of himself. "We're about to chow down."

"Oh. I need these papers signed." He waved the sheets.

"What are they?"

"Camp-At-Your-Own-Risk Contract."

"Your dad must be a little paranoid about being

sued." Nick opened the small slot in the screen and grabbed the pen and papers.

"Yeah. Some jerk threatened to sue him once over nothin'."

"Can't blame a man for being careful." Nick read the papers, signed them, and handed them back.

"Ain't that funny?" The kid shoved the contract in his jacket. "Dad said the same thing about those guys who stopped at the office a while ago."

Nick snapped to attention. "What guys?"

"Two weird lookin' dudes wanted to check out the sites." He snorted. "The jerks don't even have a tent or nothin'."

"What did your dad do?" His instincts screamed at him.

"You kiddin'? Dad only lets paying guests past the gate."

"A man can't be too careful." Were they Vargas' gunmen? "City slickers I'll bet."

"Ugly, too. And mean looking. But they didn't scare me." He stood taller and puffed out his chest. "Didn't look like no campers to me and Dad."

"Your Dad's a wise man."

"Yeah. That's my dad." The kid waved and walked away saying, "Enjoy your stay with us."

"Sure will." Nick watched to make sure he left before closing the door, and then fell against it.

He had no doubt those 'weird lookin' dudes' were after Sam. If not for the owner of this place, they would have been blasting their way through the door. Nick cursed at himself for not doing his job. Letting his guard down was a damn poor thing to do, and he knew better.

****

Samantha fumbled with the buttons to her top, trying to get them through the little holes. She could still feel the magic, the intimacy of Nick's touch. He'd left her on fire. He had been right about his abilities as a lover. Even though interrupted, he'd been fabulous. Better than she'd ever experienced. She licked her lips and tasted the Coke he'd been drinking. In all the years they'd been married, Edward hadn't made her feel all the electrifying emotions that Nick had in this brief encounter.

But now wasn't the time to make comparisons. She grabbed her backpack and went to the bedroom door to listen. The rain pounding on the tin roof stopped her from hearing much. Had Vargas' goons found her? A sudden chill made her shiver. Her arms tightened around the backpack.

You're in deep trouble when Nick finds out what you're hiding. Samantha shushed the voice in her head. He wouldn't find out about her secret until she told him.

"You can come out now."

Not wanting him to see her clutching her bag, she returned it to the closet, and then opened the bedroom door. He stood in the doorway to the bedroom with both muscular arms braced on the frame. She'd give anything to continue where they left off. The frown on his face told her that their love making had been swiped, with one blow, from his agenda. Those steel walls were up again.

Nick, the cop, was back.

The sudden loss of what they had shared overwhelmed her. She wanted to cry. But she wouldn't give him the chance to see how disappointed she felt. Or how hurt. "I couldn't hear much. Who was at the door?"

Nick explained about the paperwork.

"Thank goodness. For a moment…Let's eat, shall we?" Samantha put on the fake smile she had perfected all those years ago. She wouldn't let him know how scared she'd been. One powerful arm stopped her when she tried to squeeze past him.

"I'm sorry." He ran his fingers through his hair. "Making out like teenagers. It won't happen again."

If that's the label he wanted to place on it, so be it. There's no way she'd feel guilty about the best time she had ever spent in a man's arms, brief as it may have been. His magnetic pull got stronger every day. Fighting her attraction to him became more and more difficult.

"If that had been Vargas' gunmen, we'd be dead."

"It wasn't and we aren't." She pinched his arm to prove it to him. She sensed a tiny bit of satisfaction when he winced.

"This time."

"Really, Nick. I think you're overreacting." Admitting he could be right didn't set well with her. To avoid further scrutiny, she made a move to go around the brick wall of his chest. He grabbed her shoulders and turned her to face him. Samantha stood her ground and stared at him.

"I won't take chances with your life."

"Of course, you won't." But she would make her own decisions.

He ran his hands down to her elbows. "I can't forget protecting you is what I'm being paid to do."

"Oh, for goodness sake, Nick. We're both from the city. Who on earth is going to find us camping in the back woods of Texas? Would you think to look for us here? Will they? No. End of argument." The more she spoke the higher her voice rose.

"I think they are. Looking for us at campgrounds."

"Don't be silly. How…" Vargas got her letter. A weird feeling crawled up her back.

Nick told her what the kid had said about the two men.

"They'll be back, won't they?" The sudden realization of what he was saying hit her hard. Every nerve in her tightened. At his nod and working hard to keep her voice from shaking, she said, "What do we do now?"

"Leave."

She didn't argue. She moved around him. "Then I'd better ready the inside."

****

Ten minutes later, Nick pulled the RV out of their campsite. The blackness of the night made everything creepy. The pouring rain didn't make seeing any easier. He hadn't driven ten feet when two men in black stepped in front of the RV.

"What the hell?" He muttered, slamming on the brakes.

"Nick?" she whispered. "Guns."

"I see them."

"Turn off the engine," the meanest looking one shouted.

"Screw you," he said under his breath. "Get on the floor and stay there no matter what happens." She fell to the floor and curled in a ball.

"Do it now, or I'll shoot," yelled the other man.

Curtains moved in the trailer on the site next to them. "Hang on." Slouching down in the seat, he stomped on the gas, heading right for the men. One of the gunmen got off a couple rounds, putting two holes in the windshield. Samantha screamed and covered her head.

Shards of glass hit him on the arm. He struck one of the shooters with the bumper, throwing him into a nearby bush. He smiled when he heard him cry out. The other jumped free. Nick sat up and gunned the RV, getting to the main road in seconds. The pattern of broken glass and the inability to use the wipers made it difficult for him to see ahead. "You can come out now."

She brushed the glass off the seat and sat down. She looked at the front window. "My, God, Nick. Are you hit? One of those bullets went through your headrest."

"Naw. I slouched down. Besides, they were too busy running to take good aim."

"Poor aim or not, that was a close one. I heard a thump. Did you hit one of them?"

"He'll limp for a while." He cursed the rain and poor visibility under his breath. "We've got to park this thing."

He drove until he found a large industrial building. He checked to make sure no one followed. Satisfied no lights were visible, he pulled in the driveway and around to the back. Nick smiled.

"Just what we need." He drove the front end under the overhang and turned off the motor to listen. The terrific downpour of the rain beating on the corrugated tin roof of the overhang was the only sound he heard.

Nick motioned for her to move to the inside of the RV. Once inside, he shut the folding privacy door into the living area. They were safe for now.

"That should help keep some of the chill off." He picked a piece of glass off his jacket. "Let's grab a quick sandwich, then you'd better get some shut-eye. We need to be out of here before this place opens." He motioned to the front window. "We'll need to stop at a glass repair shop in the morning."

"You need to get some rest, too."

"I want to keep watch for a while." They weren't followed, but he wasn't about to get caught with his pants unhitched again.

Nick's mind was already churning with questions. How did they find them so fast? He'd only told the captain about the RV that day. Had Mike been listening to his conversation? Nick rubbed his face with his hands. Having doubts about his old friend and partner tore him apart.

****

The first thing in the morning, Nick cleared the remaining broken glass from the front window.

Samantha came to the front when he was picking up the last of the glass. "You didn't think the window had been damaged enough?"

"We don't want people calling the cops and asking questions we don't want to answer." He motioned to the two holes in the head rest. "Can you find something to cover these?"

She went to the back and came out with a hand towel and some pins. She covered the holes. "There that should do it."

A half hour later, sitting at breakfast, he asked the

waitress where they could get the window repaired. It took all morning to get the windshield fixed. Soon they were headed south with the windows down. The fumes from the sealer the guy had used were giving him a cheap high.

It had been a hell of a short night and a long morning. He decided not to mention the attack to his captain.

Worrying half the night about Mike didn't compare to spending the rest of it visualizing Samantha sleeping naked. Even now, all he thought about was how great she felt in his arms and the sweet catches of her breath when he touched her. Man. All her little wiggles and moans were getting him into a lot of trouble. He struck the palm of his hand against the steering wheel.

Enough. Damnation.

"Is there something wrong?"

He jerked his head toward her. "No. Why?"

"You just struck the wheel." She glanced at the wheel and back at him.

"I did? I mean…Yes, I did. I…have to make a phone call." He looked back at the road. He wasn't about to tell her his thoughts, his fantasies. Better to let her believe sex between them wouldn't happen again. And it wouldn't.

"Are you going to call Captain Bianco?"

"No. Detective Bauer." He needed to check on Mike.

"Is she your girlfriend?"

"Jealous?" he teased.

Samantha stared straight ahead and ignored him.

Nick wanted to lie to her and tell her yes; but after last night, he didn't want her to believe him an unfaithful jerk or a womanizer. That was his father, not him.

"Just a fellow officer and Mike's current partner."

"I liked her. She seemed nice. And well trained."

He nodded. "I'll call her when we stop to eat lunch."

Samantha nodded and stared out the window. "This part of the state is different, isn't it?"

"Less prairie grass and more greasewood."

"Just what is greasewood? I've heard of it but never seen it before."

"See those low shrub-like things?" Nick pointed to some along the road. When she nodded, he added, "That's greasewood."

They were traveling south along a state route, electing to leave the interstate a few miles out of Midland.

They stopped near Fort Stockton for lunch. Nick had hoped for another Cindy Lou to brighten their day. Instead the waitress turned out to be a tall, lanky inexperienced teenager.

After they finished a quick lunch of taco salads and iced tea, Nick excused himself to use the pay phone.

"Detective Bauer," Amy answered.

"How's the cutest detective in the precinct?"

"This has to be O'Reilly feeding me a line of bull."

"Now, sweetheart." Nick laughed. He knew she was making the same screwed up face she always made when he teased her.

"What's up? Are you still camping? In an RV, right?"

What the hell! Only the captain knew, or that is what he thought. "Where did you hear that?"

"Mike told me."

"Now where would Mike get such an idea?" Not from the captain for sure. Nick's suspicions of Mike grew.

"He was having a powwow with the captain when you called. Neither of them could picture you camping. I must admit, that's a far stretch for me, too."

Nick's heart jumped in his throat. "Are you alone?"

"That would be affirmative. Why?"

"You sure no one's around?" Namely, Mike.

"Jeesh, Detective. Is all that fresh air rattling your brain? Making you paranoid?" Amy chuckled.

"No," he shouted, ramming his fingers through his hair. Realizing Samantha and others were staring, Nick turned to face the wall and lowered his voice. "Does anyone else know?"

"Well…I don't think so. What's the big secret?"

"I'm trying to keep the prosecutor's star witness alive. That's hard to do when the whole department knows where I am."

"It's just the picture of you camping. But you're right. I'm sorry."

"The fewer people who know, the safer our witness. You're one person I thought I could trust. That's why I called you." Nick pinched the bridge of his nose.

"Thank you. I appreciate the confidence. I doubt that Mike said anything because he made me promise to keep it quiet."

How many others had Mike told to do the same? At least three people at the precinct knew their plans. Nick rammed his fingers through his hair once again. "Where's Mike?"

"He's getting coffee. Why? You need him for something?"

"No. I'll catch him later." *Like when I get home.*

"I'll tell him you called. He'll be sorry he missed you."

"Okay if we keep this call between the two of us?"

Amy hesitated before saying, "You can count on me."

"Thanks." *That's what I'm hoping.* But could he? Right now, the only person he trusted was himself.

"Here's my home phone in case you need me."

Nick pulled out his faithful notebook and jotted the number down. "Thanks."

"You be careful, O'Reilly."

"Always." Nick hung up and stared out the restaurant window wondering what to do now. The RV wasn't as safe as it had been. One thing he knew for sure. No more lusting after Samantha. Not after this wakeup-or-get-killed call.

Chapter 11

Samantha studied the tourist flyers she'd picked up at the restaurant while they continued on their journey. "Here's a small out-of-the-way campsite we might be interested in."

Nick shook his head. "No advertised one." He thought for a minute. "We'll head south. Look for a dumpy campground."

"Dumpy?" She shuddered. "Why must we stay in such a place? There are plenty of nicer, secluded campgrounds."

"We want an unpopular one."

Samantha stared at him for a moment. "Why are you so moody? What did you find out from Detective Bauer?"

"Not much."

"If anything happened back home, I need to know."

He didn't answer. He seemed lost in another world.

She touched his arm. "Nick?"

He jumped. "You okay?" He checked the mirrors and the area around them.

Samantha couldn't speak, trying to cope with the warmth seeping into her fingertips, up her arm, and settling in her stomach. Once more little butterflies fluttered. Samantha brought her hand to her midsection. After what had happened last night, she wasn't surprised at her reaction.

"Why did you grab my arm?" He rubbed the spot. "Jeesh, Sam. You scared the crap out of me. Did you see something?"

"No. I asked you a question."

"I guess my mind wandered." He reached for a Tootsie Roll in his pocket, opened it and jammed it into his mouth.

"Really? You think so?" She turned and leaned toward him. "What's bothering you? Don't forget I'm in this charade, too."

He swallowed his candy and let out a big sigh. "I think I know why those gunmen found us."

Samantha put her hand on her chest. Did Nick know about the letter to Vargas? "How?" she managed to get out.

"People at the precinct know we're traveling in this RV."

Relief rushed through her. He didn't know her secret. Samantha took a deep breath and let it out slowly. "Did you tell anyone?"

"Just the captain. I didn't know Mike was in the captain's office at the time. Mike has a big mouth."

"Is that bad? After all, he's your partner."

"That he is." Nick shrugged. "Mike was in on Plan A. He's also laughing his as…head off about me camping. He told Bauer. Maybe he's told others."

"How does that connect to the men finding us last night?"

"The mole in the department would've rushed to inform Vargas." Nick rubbed the back of his neck. "He knows. Otherwise, why would those two men have shot at us?"

Her letter led that murderer right to them. How dumb could she be? Samantha knew she should tell him about the letter, but she couldn't. "Can Detective Bauer be trusted?"

"I think so, but right now, I'm leery of everyone. The only one I trust is the captain. We go back a long way."

At last, he'd offered information about himself. "How long?"

"Forever." Nick stepped on the accelerator a little harder, making the RV fly down the highway. "Let's see if we can find that secluded dump."

"I'll keep my eyes open." Samantha leaned back in her seat, watching for signs along the road ahead. Nick wasn't a trusting person, yet Captain Bianco had earned his trust. And she hadn't. Would Nick ever trust her that much? Instinct told her his life had been a hard one. It left him vulnerable on the one hand and hard as stone on the other. Samantha didn't know if they would be together long enough for her to earn the respect he required. There were only seven days to trial, which left seven days for her to accomplish this.

Any confidence he had in her would be gone when he found out about the letter *and* the cross. She had to tell him, but she dreaded the explosion that would follow. What could she say?

My husband is dead because he ordered me to hide a cross belonging to Vargas. Oh, by the way. I'm carrying that precious family heirloom in my backpack. Would you like to take a peek? No. She didn't think so. Not yet.

She should have insisted Edward move out after she found him in the act of fencing stolen jewelry. Now he was dead, and she possessed what Vargas wanted. Nick was already suspicious and would never believe she intended to give the cross to the D.A.

****

Two nights later, stuffed from overeating at a local restaurant, Nick felt more himself. He hated that the word was out about the RV. To make matters worse, there was talk of Vargas being released on bail earlier than expected. He received the bad news this morning when he called his boss. From now on, it became absolutely necessary to keep their location a secret. Vargas' gunmen found them once; they'd find them again. Soon they would have to switch to an unknown Plan C.

Last night they'd found the perfect spot a few miles outside Alpine to camp. The sign was faded and back from the road. They almost missed it. Only ten campsites and set back in a secluded area. He hoped they could do as well tonight. Nick yawned. He was exhausted. A full day behind the wheel would do that to a man.

He relaxed when they found a private campground outside of Del Rio. This one was fenced in on all sides except for the river flowing close by. No hired gunmen would think to look for them here. If they did, it wouldn't be an easy entry.

Leaning against the front of the RV, Nick watched Samantha sitting in a lawn chair with her trusty backpack by her feet. After having spent most of her money, why keep it so close? The woman could be a mystery at times. Right now, she looked peaceful and relaxed, staring at the horizon. He headed toward her, pulled a quarter from his pocket and flipped the coin into her lap. She glanced down and then at him.

She picked up the quarter. Look at it, then at him. "Lose something?"

"A piece of silver for your thoughts?" He sat down in the lawn chair next to her.

She smiled and turned back to gaze at the stars.

"They must be good ones."

"They are. It's so beautiful and quiet here."

"Still might run into a rattlesnake or a copperhead," Nick teased.

"Where?" Samantha jerked her feet up onto her chair.

Nick chuckled. "I didn't say I saw one."

"Oh, you…you—"

"Tut. Tut. Tut." Nick wiggled his index finger at her. "Remember. You're a lady."

"You're incorrigible."

"I try." Nick didn't want to interrupt the tranquility of this beautiful night, but he needed to learn more about her relationship with her husband and with Vargas. He needed answers for his own self-preservation. "I've been thinking about your house with the hidden hallways. How did you end up with the family mansion?"

She turned and stared at him. "Where did that come from?"

Nick slouched down in his chair. "Just curious."

"My grandfather left it to me, his only grandchild. He's the one who introduced me to its secrets."

"Some inheritance."

"I love my house." Samantha spread her arms out, "and I love this place, but staying here longer is out of the question, I know."

Nick nodded. They couldn't take the risk. He watched day turn into night. They sat in silence. The sun disappeared and the moon came out. No fire, just the stars painting pictures in the beautiful sky. He inhaled the sweet fragrance of fresh air. He could get used to this camping idea. Samantha's soft voice interrupted his wandering thoughts.

"My parents would hate this place." She motioned with her arm. "Too laid back for them. Large hotels and enclosed pools are more their style."

"Real highbrows, huh?" She had fit that mold a few days ago, but this trip was changing her. Nick liked the new Samantha. It got harder every day to remember he was a cop with a job to do and she a socialite with tons of money. None of that mattered right now.

"They aren't the outdoor type and never will be."

"Were you? Before this happened?" He had his doubts.

"Whenever I was home from boarding school, I'd slip out through the secret passageway and sit under the big old maple tree on our back lawn and dream."

"What does a gal, with everything money can buy, hope for?" He couldn't begin to imagine what a wealthy girl like her might want.

Samantha sighed. "Back then I dreamed of finding the love of my life and raising a family."

"Was Edward that love?" Did she flinch? In the darkness, he couldn't tell. Did she hate Thorne enough to help Vargas kill him? He didn't like to think of her as an accomplice to murder. Damn. He had to keep an open mind.

"I told you I never loved him. He was a way to hurt my parents. It came back to haunt me in the end."

"Oh?" Nick sat up straight in his chair. Had he been right all along? The sudden ache around his heart made him hope he wasn't.

"Using the passageway started when I was about twelve. I used it to sneak out to meet Sarah, my best friend. Mother didn't like Sarah or any of my friends. I escaped many times over the years to meet her and others. We'd go to the movies and places, but most of all we enjoyed spending time dreaming together." Samantha smiled. "We continued doing girlie things during our college years. Vacations and summers, too. Those were happy times." She wore a contented smile.

She turned in her seat to face Nick. "That's how I met Edward. One afternoon Sarah and I stopped at Thorne's Gems to look at the pretty jewelry. Edward flirted with me and asked me out. For six weeks, the sneaking around and enjoying each other was exciting. Eloping and getting out of the control of my parents was sensational." Samantha stared up at the star-studded sky. "In the end, I recognized everything we did...pure rebellion on my part."

"One you paid dearly for, I gather."

"Yes. I lived to regret it." She looked down at her hands.

Could that be her incentive to help Vargas kill Edward? "I'll bet the crap hit the fan when you announced your happy union."

"You might say that. My mother raged for days." Samantha turned back to sit on the edge of her chair.

"I'll bet." Nick watched her for any sign of guilt and found none.

"Oh, but they made us have a formal wedding. Eloping's not socially correct, you know. My parents walked around like zombies all afternoon with grins frozen on their faces." She smiled. "Still, I gloated over my success for days. I had done something they had no say in and couldn't change."

"Your marriage made a big splash in the papers."

"Having the Chadwick name publicized in the society column is important to my mother in particular. Never to me."

"So how was marital bliss?" He needed to know. Not for personal reasons, but for the job. *Yeah, right. Who in hell am I kidding?*

"The early years were okay. I was free of my parents' rule and living in my own house. Edward and I were friends and got along…okay." She shrugged, "We didn't have a true romantic love relationship. He never cared what I did. He was really wrapped up in making a success of his business."

"What changed?"

"Edward. He started telling me where I could and couldn't go. Wanted to know my every move. It was my parents all over again."

"Maybe that is when he learned of his father's other partner. Maybe he had been threatened. Maybe he was trying to protect you." Maybe Edward was a better man than he thought.

Samantha thought for a moment. "You may be right. I didn't know about Vargas either." She tapped her nails on the chair arm. "Do you think that may have been the reason for the change?"

"Very possible." Knowing the cunning of Vargas, Nick thought that he had come up with the exact reason. Threats on family can make a man or woman act abnormal.

Nick hated to keep interrogating her, but he had to know once and for all if she aided in her husband's murder. "How long were you married?"

"Almost four years." Samantha sat back in the seat and crossed her legs.

"When did you learn he was fencing jewels?"

"Two months before he died. Edward was working late. He claimed he was filling a special order."

"Did he get special orders often?"

"I really didn't pay much attention to his business. He spent weeks working late into the evenings. I had no reason to question his work."

"What changed your mind?"

"One night I got bored, and I decided to visit him. Edward was in the workroom and didn't hear me enter. I really enjoyed watching a master at work. Then it hit me. He was *removing* stones from a huge assortment of jewelry."

"What happened then?"

"We argued. He'd never spoken to me like that before. I went back home, steaming angry and calling him all kinds of names."

"Why didn't you turn him in to the police?"

"I thought about it, but he *was* my husband. I couldn't turn him in without getting his side." Samantha inhaled a deep breath and let it out. "Edward's dad had died a couple months before." She turned to Nick. "That's when Vargas started making threats."

"You knew for a fact Edward had been threatened?"

"Yes. Vargas threatened to kill Edward's mother and me if my husband didn't continue his father's work." She shuddered. "The idea of it gives me the chills."

"Want me to get your sweater?" He'd be shaking in his shoes, too, knowing a killer could end his life at any time. Vargas did really well at blackmailing people. He couldn't wait to see the man sentenced to life in prison. No one deserved it more.

She hugged herself and started pacing. "Edward not only inherited the jewelry business, but he also acquired a silent partner. He claimed he knew nothing of this silent partnership until Vargas approached him with the same kind of threats right after our marriage."

"Edward was a partner, too, right?"

"Yes. He swore he didn't know about Vargas until he became a partner."

Nick shook his head. "It would be impossible to hide a fencing operation right under the nose of your son and partner."

"That's what I thought, but we didn't discuss Edward's business. Ever." Samantha hugged herself again. "I guess criminals don't advertise their illegal businesses."

"Not as a rule." Nick chuckled. Not any that he knew. "If Thorne was a victim, why not call in the police?"

"Edward claimed Vargas had the police on his payroll. After what's happened to me, I know he was right."

"I agree." Nick would bet his next paycheck Vargas had a direct line to the precinct. "The question is *who*?"

"Vargas always knows where the police have me hidden. That can't be a coincidence."

Nick shook his head. "No argument there. What happened next?"

"Edward wanted me to give him two months to end his business with Vargas."

"And you agreed just like that." Nick snapped his fingers. "Your fairytale continues." A cynical smile twisted his face.

"Fairytale!" Samantha shook her head. "I agreed to give him time, but…" She looked up at the stars. "From that night, Edward and I never slept…ah…he used the guest bedroom."

"You kicked him out of your bed?" The tone of Nick's voice rose.

"Yes. I couldn't sleep with a crook. I told Edward to go to the police, but he was frightened. He promised he would figure out a way to get free of Vargas. Six weeks later, he did. Vargas killed him. I live with the guilt of not telling him about the passageway. Maybe he would have been able to use it to get away."

"Maybe. Maybe not." With a determined Vargas on his tail, he wouldn't have had the opportunity to escape.

"Before Edward died, I found a small velvet bag in our safe, containing a jeweled cross. When I asked him about the beautiful piece, he told me it belonged to him. He gave it to me to keep safe. The very next day I heard him talking on the phone to Vargas. That's when I discovered the real owner."

"Where is the cross now?"

"In a safe place." She got up, picked up her chair and headed toward the RV. "Good night."

****

The next morning, sitting at the table sipping her

tea, Samantha cursed herself for not telling Nick the whole story. She should have told him that first day. The fear of him confiscating the cross and accusing her of helping her husband had stopped her. The cross was her ticket to safety or at least that is what she had thought at the time. She no longer believed it. Vargas would kill her once he got his property in his dirty hands.

Now, Nick was suspicious. He hadn't said two words to her since he woke up. A sudden unbelievable thought struck her.

"Did he believe I was involved in Edward's fencing business? Did he think I killed Edward, too?"

The thought made her ill. It hurt to think she fell for a man who thought her capable of murder and may even consider her a prime suspect.

"Oh. No." The words blasted out of her mouth. Had she fallen for Nick? They'd only known each other nine days. It couldn't be possible.

"Something wrong?" Nick yelled from outside.

Samantha forgot he was fiddling with whatever men did to engines. "Just thinking out loud," she yelled back.

Love? She longed for him to make love to her. Was that love or lust? Their passion ignited like a flame to dry grass the other night. Her feelings for him were foreign to her. Her parents had always insisted she didn't love Edward, but she'd bite off her tongue before she'd admit they were right.

Samantha held her head in her hands. What a fine kettle of caviar she managed to get herself into. And she hated the salty stuff. As if running for her life from campground to campground wasn't enough, the man she might be falling in love with suspected her of murder. Could she be intimate with someone who thought her capable of such a crime? She knew he desired her and fought against his feelings. She understood his situation. But what about her?

All she ever wanted to do was to control her own life. Whether she was sent to prison, killed, or fell in love, she'd lose that which was most precious to her—freedom.

Chapter 12

Samantha admired the Texas countryside. The land shifted from mountains to plains to pastureland. Nick managed to travel every direction possible in the state to keep her safe.

Every day, finding a remote place for target practice fell on her shoulders, while Nick tended to the driving. It was difficult to know where to locate sandbanks and other remote spots.

"Let's try this dirt road. I don't think it gets much traffic."

"Let's take a look-see." He made a right-hand turn on to the half grass, half dirt road.

"Over there. See! A perfect spot." She pointed straight ahead where the road ended at the base of a large bank that had been washed away by years of rain.

Nick stopped the RV and set up the target. "Ready?"

"I feel lucky today." She smiled and got ready to fire the gun. It felt more comfortable in her hands than it had the first few times she practiced.

"Okay, Sam. Ready when you are." He stepped back to watch.

Samantha set her legs and readied the gun the way he had taught her. The first shot hit the outside edge of the target. "Darn."

"That's okay, Sam. Take your time. Don't hurry

the shot," Nick instructed.

She relaxed. Took a deep breath and let it out. Aimed. Fired.

Thump! The bullet shot through the paper target and into the bank.

She turned, "Did I hit the little circle?" He grinned. She looked at the target again. "I hit it! Yes. I hit it." Samantha jumped up and down, raised her arms, shouting, "I did it! I hit the center!"

She ran over and jumped on Nick with both feet around his waist, her arms around his neck and gave him a big smack on the lips. He wrapped his arms around her and gave her the kiss she had wanted, needed.

The butterflies fluttered in her stomach, and her heart did a couple quick beats before thundering in her chest. He held her so close she could feel his heart keeping sync with hers. A moan rumbled in her throat, her accomplishment forgotten. Samantha slid down Nick's body until her feet touched the ground, still clinging to his neck and mouth. He broke the kiss and gave her several quick kisses and then settled into an open-mouthed, hungry kiss. She could taste the Tootsie Roll on his tongue and smell the citrus odor that always flowed about him. How she had longed for this moment. She wanted him to make love to her right there in the sandbank. Her need for him grew with every nibble he made on her lips.

"Woof. Woof. Woof."

Nick pushed her behind him, gun ready and pointed at the sandbank. There, an angry German Shepard stood, barking at them. She smiled, but Nick did not. Nick, the cop, had returned.

"Let's move. We've been here too long." He grabbed the target and headed toward the RV. He pointed to her hand. "Put that away."

Samantha hadn't realized she was still holding the weapon. If she hadn't been hanging on the handle, she might have pulled the trigger in her excitement. She could have shot Nick. Or herself. It gave her a reality check, warning her to be more careful.

Back on the road again, the silent treatment was back in force. Let him be in one of his moods. She, instead, congratulated herself for her perfect shot. Practice had made her perfect and she could only thank Nick for insisting she learn to use his weapon. His actions proved he was proud of her.

Her mother, on the other hand, would have had a fainting spell if she knew her daughter had learned to use a gun, not to mention hitting the target. Such actions were 'undignified.' If those two men at the campsite ever caught up with them again, she'd be real glad Nick had insisted she learn how to use his Glock.

Later, they went through a drive-through at a fast food restaurant to grab some hamburgers and fries for dinner. Nick drove to a nearby mall to park and eat. They sat at the small table in the RV in silence. Unable to stand it a minute longer, Samantha put down her hamburger.

"Okay. What's wrong Nick? You haven't spoken a word to me since this morning."

He took a bite of his burger and stared at her. She waited, staring back at him.

"What happened earlier shouldn't and can't happen again."

"What? Me hitting the center of the target for the

first time? I thought that was what I was supposed to do." She knew that wasn't what he meant, but she wanted him to say the words. His raised eyebrow acknowledged the fact that she knew.

"The kiss. Okay? If that had been—"

"Vargas' man instead of a dog we'd be dead," she mimicked. "I've heard it before." Same old thing she was tired of hearing. "Why can't you just say you enjoyed it and let it go?" Her voice got louder with every word.

He put his burger down and looked at her. "I'm a cop hired to protect you. That's my job." He ran his fingers through his hair. "Kissing you, though pleasurable, is not part of the deal."

Admitting he enjoyed it gave her hope and made it easier to calm herself and lower her voice. "Nick, we're adults. It was the excitement of the moment. I was happy. You were happy for me. Is that any reason to not talk to me?"

"No. It's just…Hell. I could kick myself in the bal…behind for letting things get out of hand." He ran his fingers through his hair once again before grabbing a couple fries and stuffing them in his mouth. "My stupidity isn't your fault. It's just so damn hard to resist you."

"Why is that wrong?" She wanted him to desire her. After all, she'd never felt this way about a man before.

"Being around you, touching you, kissing you interferes with my job. My concentration. Nothing or no one has ever done that to me before." He rubbed his face with his hands. "Besides, I've never kissed a woman I'm guarding."

"And I've never kissed a cop."

****

An hour later, they pulled into The Mirror Pond Campground, located around a huge man-made pond. They chose the most remote site available once again. He didn't want neighbors near in case of a shoot-out. Facing the entrance to the campground and having a direct exit route—perfect site.

They spent some time walking around the campground to check things out. They were quite isolated with just a couple other campers on the other side of the pond. Satisfied they were safe for the time being, they took a blanket and sat by the water. Nick laid back and rested his head on his folded arms. Samantha sat, legs curled beneath her, arguing with herself about whether to tell Nick about the cross. She decided against it, unable to ruin this flawless evening. Sensing his gaze on her, she looked at him and smiled. "It's nice here."

"Yeah. Nice."

"Watching water has always fascinated me," Samantha whispered. "Some water travels slow and easy. Some rushes angrily, slapping and curling around anything in its way. This pond, however, doesn't appear to move at all."

Nick sighed. "Reminds me of my life. The angry slapping and curling part."

Samantha stare at the moon's reflection on the water. Mr. Closed-Mouth-About-Me mentioned something about his life again. She wanted to learn more about him—his childhood, his family, his likes and dislikes. Everything.

Nick reached in his pocket and pulled out his

favorite candy. "Want one?"

"Not just now. Thank you." She watched him unwrap it, stuff it in his mouth and rest his head on his arms again. "Why do you eat so many of those?"

He shrugged again. "To stop myself from smoking."

"You gave up one habit for another?" Samantha smiled.

He patted his supply of Tootsie Rolls. "This one's healthier."

"Aren't you afraid you'll put on weight? I'd gain forty pounds"—Samantha touched her waist—"right here."

"Naw. Not in the genes."

"Are your parents thin?" She looked toward the lake, daring not to look at him for fear he'd stop talking.

"Were." He took one arm from behind his head and pulled on his earlobe. "Ma's gone."

"Oh, I'm so sorry, Nick. What about your father."

Nick sat up and wrapped his arms around his knees. "Don't know. Don't care."

Whatever happened between Nick and his father must have been drastic. It still hurt him.

Thankfully, she still had her father and mother. Though they traveled around the world and weren't home much, she loved them both. Mother could be a pain with the importance she placed on appearances, but she was still hers.

"Tell me about your mom."

"Playing shrink again, Doc?"

"I would really like to know." Nick looked at her for a long moment. She didn't know what expression he could see in the moonlight, but it must have satisfied him.

"She was tall, thin and…special."

"You loved her," Samantha added when he remained quiet. Several moments passed before he spoke.

"Yeah."

"What is the nicest memory you have of her?"

Nick looked out at the water for a long time. Then he spoke in such a low voice she leaned toward him to hear.

"Talking and dreaming with her about our future."

In those few words, she could feel the loneliness in the child and the hopelessness in the mother. What must he have endured? She could only guess with her privileged background.

"I'd like to hear about those dreams, if you care to share them with me."

"It's hard." His voice cracked. The muscles in his arms jumped with the force he put on them, gripping his hands into fists. He stared into the night.

Her heart went out to him. To the boy who had lost the one person he loved and to the man who still mourned. She touched his arm, pleased when he left it there.

"I lived a different life from yours. We were dirt poor. Ma worked her butt off in the local factory doing a man's work for little pay. She'd come home at night so tired she leaned on anything she could grab to help her walk, but she'd always spend time with me. Sometimes she'd just listen and let me talk. Ma often fell asleep during those times." Nick smiled. "Other times, we'd sit out on the pile of old lumber we used as a porch. She'd rock and I'd sit at her feet. I still haven't figured out how she managed everything."

Samantha listened and realized how privileged her life had been. She had all the food she wanted and a grand mansion full of history for a home. She complained about being controlled and wanting freedom, but having both parents wanting the best for her beat the suffering he and his mother had lived through.

I will never feel ungrateful for my family and the protected life they gave me again.

"Her love for you was stronger than anything else." She squeezed his forearm. He wrapped his fingers around her hand. "She sounds like a wonderful woman."

"She was." He blinked several times and turned away. She still heard the sniff he tried to cover up with a cough. "If only our favorite dream had come true while she lived."

"Dreams may take a while, but they will come true."

"Not this one. Why am I telling you all this?" He shook his head.

"Because I'd like to know the woman who made you the man you are today." She didn't speak again and waited. After a several minutes went by, he continued.

"Her one dream was to get me out of the slums. Ma dreamed of the perfect life—a nice clean white house with a normal porch for us to sit on. We laughed over the huge old maple tree we'd have in our big yard." He glanced at her. "Probably resembled your favorite tree." He turned to stare back into the night.

"There'd be a tree house and a tire swing for me.

She wanted a pulley clothesline to hang our clothes in the fresh clean air instead of the smoke filled stinkin' stuff in the slums. Most of all she wanted me to have a dog."

"What a wonderful dream. She wanted a special life for her only child." And he was breaking her heart.

Nick looked at her. "I wanted it for her, too." He picked up a pebble nearby and whipped it into the pond. It skipped across the water radiating ripples with each hop.

"For a few minutes each day, she took you out of the slums and put you both in a happier place—one you shared together. What an extraordinary gift she gave you. It was her way of giving you a piece of heaven and a beautiful dream for your life."

"Damn it! Don't you see? She left me." Nick jammed his fingers in his hair.

"*Never* by choice. You were her sole purpose for living."

"Every dream died with her." He whipped another stone.

"No. They didn't." She rose on her knees to look him in the eyes. "You have accomplished exactly what she dreamed for you."

"Yeah, sure," he said in disbelief.

"Yes, you have." She placed her hands, one on each side of his face. "Where do you live?"

He looked at her as if she had just sprouted a horn in the middle of her head. "A few miles outside of Albany. Why?"

"Your mother dreamed of you living in a safe neighborhood. Yours is, right?" He nodded his head. "You are alive and well. You have a good job. You are respected. And I'll bet you have that loveable dog."

"Cody. A mongrel like me." He pulled back from her and flipped another stone. "But what good is it without Ma there to see it all?" Moisture glistened in eyes that had turned a deep brown.

"Yes, she is. She's here." Samantha put her hand over Nick's heart and then to his head. "She knows. She's probably the proudest mom in heaven." Tears were forming in her eyes. Her voice cracked and she smiled at him.

"You think so?" A teardrop trickled down his cheek.

Samantha wiped it with her thumb. "I truly believe."

"Oh. God. I miss her so." Tears filled his eyes.

Unable to resist any longer, Samantha wrapped him in the biggest hug she could manage. He hesitated for a moment before he hauled her close and buried his face in her neck. His body shook with the sobs he was trying to hold back.

"Let it out. It's time to release the pain." And forgive his mother for leaving him.

"I...I don't—

"Your mother wouldn't want you to live your life with this kind of hurt." Silently weeping, she held him close to her breasts.

****

Nick had no idea how long he had been crying like a wet-nosed kid. He'd never broken down in front of anyone. Not even Captain Bianco, his mentor and the closest to a real father he'd ever known. Feeling thoroughly drained and a whole lot foolish, he forced himself to raise his head.

Samantha pulled away to look at him. "Feeling better?"

He wiped his eyes with the back of his hand. "Men don't blat like babies."

"Then they should." She cupped his cheek with her hand.

In his head, he called himself all kinds of names. What a fool he'd been to talk about his mother to Samantha, a woman who never had a financial worry in her life. Hell. He never felt this embarrassed. "I can't believe I told you about—"

"Your mother? Your dreams?" She patted his cheek and lowered her hand.

"Yeah. You must think I'm some kind of sentimental fool." Or an emotional jerk.

"On the contrary. You're a man who loves and misses his mother. There's no fault in that." She smiled up at him. "It says a lot about you. I like what I'm hearing."

Nick did a quick surveillance of the camping area. No sign of movement anywhere. The other campsites were dark. Beside the moon, the only glow came from the light near the office reflecting off the pond. His Glock was secure and handy. Safe for now.

He wanted to make love to this woman, but he couldn't. Not now, but a quick kiss of gratitude would be okay. Nick took her by the arm and pulled her close. He ran his fingers through her strawberry blonde ringlets, down her smooth neck and cupped her chin. He brought her lips to his intending to give her a gentle peck. Keep cool, he kept telling himself. You're on the job.

The hunger he sensed in her put a crack in every

good intention he possessed. She placed her hand on the back of his head, pulling him closer. When she slipped her tongue into his mouth, his body shook with a shiver that ended in his groin area. He tried to pull back, but her grip on his head held him in place. Knowing he'd hate himself later, Nick couldn't stop the crazy urges in his lower body from bursting forth and taking what she so willingly offered.

Leaning over her, Nick kissed her with such intensity it rocked him to his toes. She was soft and willing in his arms. He felt like he'd come home at last when she curled herself around him. The need to taste her soft velvet skin overwhelmed him. He began to pull her top off. She grabbed it, ripped it off and tossed it aside. Then, she reached for her bra.

"No. Let me do it." He moved her hand away. He took time to check out the campgrounds, while unsnapping her bra and tossing it on the blanket. "We shouldn't be doing this," he murmured.

She gripped his face with both hands. "Please…don't…stop," she moaned.

Samantha's beautiful firm breasts glowing in the moonlight got his attention and made his heart skip a beat. Caressing each of them turned him into a breathless horny teen. No way could he stop now.

"Perfect," he muttered, panting.

"Take off your shirt."

Before he could move, she grabbed the front of his flannel shirt, popped the buttons, and chucked it away. He helped her pull off his T-shirt. She ran her hands over his chest, caressing him. He could feel every goose pimple covering his chest and arms.

"Beautiful muscles."

He lowered his head and kissed rings around her nipples. Samantha moaned, making him grow harder. "You like that?" He ran his tongue around first one breast then the other, taking pains to avoid the hard nubs raised and ready for him.

"Oh. Yes," she breathed, her head thrashing. "You're making me crazy." She raised her chest to push her breasts closer to his mouth.

"Is this what you want, baby?" Nick gave a growl of satisfaction when at last his mouth settled over her nipple. Her whimpers were music to his ears. His heart swelled. Pleasuring her did double duty on him. Samantha wiggled, sending lightning currents to his male organ. If he lost control, he'd be done before he began. This must be heaven, he thought. His need for her grew with each second that passed.

Spurred on by her need, he pulled off her jeans and panties. He began caressing and kissing his way down her perfect body covered with baby soft skin. He worked his way down each of her beautiful legs, stopping to caress every curve and valley.

When he cupped her, she cried, "Please. Oh. Please." She pushed harder against his hand. Then he slipped a finger into her hot, wet folds. She bucked uncontrollably when he slipped a second finger in and began working them, stroke after stroke. Her readiness for him sent a warm heat to a vital part of him, igniting a fire so hot he began to sweat. Samantha stiffened. She throbbed against his fingers, turning him white hot.

"Oh, Baby." Panting, Nick thought he'd burst, feeling the rush he hadn't felt in forever. But he couldn't. Not yet. She deserved better. She needed to feel special over and over again. He would do this for her or die trying.

He brought her to the edge several times, listening and loving her reactions to the sweet whimpers and groans of pleasure he gave her. The enjoyment he received in turn couldn't be measured by any standards. No woman had ever responded this beautifully to his loving. When he brought her over the edge for the last time, he kissed her to cover the scream she released. Then she went limp in his arms. He held her and comforted her with sweet kisses and gentle caressing. Somehow, he managed to maintain enough strength to control himself. Nick smiled down at her.

"And you bragged you didn't whimper."

A smile lit up her eyes. "Sometimes it's necessary."

He pulled her close and gave her a long open-mouth kiss that came straight from his heart.

"Hmmm," she moaned. "Wonderful, but you didn't—"

"This one was for you."

"But I want you—"

"Shush." Nick leaned down to rest his forehead on hers.

****

Samantha wrapped her arms around his neck and held him close. The hot open mouth kiss she placed on his lips worked. She could feel the smoldering flames rekindle in him. "You are overdressed." She got on her knees and tugged off the western boots he still wore from their clothes exchange at the airport. She made short work of undoing his jeans and pulling them off along with his briefs. "Now you are dressed the way I like."

Nick smiled. "Is that so?"

Samantha didn't miss Nick, the cop, doing his duty. Always on the alert. She would fix that.

She pushed Nick back on the blanket and straddled him. He reached up to touch her breasts. She slapped his hands. "None of that stuff, Mister. It's my turn to torture you." She leaned over him, her nipples gently tickling his chest. He moaned. "We're going to have some fun, *Stud*."

She decided to tease him by rubbing the length of her body back and forth on his. Nick no longer looked relaxed. The smile he wore disappeared. He was gripping the blanket, making every muscle in his arms work. She felt the heat rising in her own body, but she wasn't finished. "Do you like this?"

"Witch." He muttered.

Samantha smiled. "And don't you forget it." She nibbled on the buds on his nipples. He jerked. She gloated. He moaned when she blew a gentle breath in his ear and ran her tongue in and around it.

She sat up to run her hands over his stomach in search of his male organ. His penis jerked at her touch. Laughing, she wrapped her hand around him and began a slow up and down motion of loving torture.

"Good, huh?" She enjoyed playing with him, but her desire for him grew by the second.

"CIA…could…ooooh," he moaned, "use…you.

She increased the rhythm.

"Holy sh…crap.

"Is this what you want?" She increased the rhythm again.

"No…I…you." The sweat ran off his face. He tried to flip her over on her back, but she managed to keep him right where she wanted him. He wiggled and thrashed around to the point where his head lay in the grass.

All the while her hormones were flipping off the charts. She was dripping with perspiration, too. She didn't know how much longer she could keep this up before she exploded.

"Is everything all right, *Stud*?" She tried to act surprised but couldn't stop smiling.

"You're about to find out." He grabbed her around the waist and shoulders and flipped her beneath him. "You've had your fun, now it's my turn."

Samantha couldn't suppress the moan that escaped her when Nick took his time entering her. She ran her hands over his back, taking pleasure in feeling his muscles move while he held himself above her. Waves of excitement surged through her. Nothing could compare to those overpowering feelings. She shut her eyes to amplify the emotions rippling inside her. No one had ever been so careful, yet demanding, with her.

Or shown her such consideration.

Or made her feel this precious.

"Look at me, Sam." She opened her eyes. "So beautiful," he whispered.

"Yours...black," she panted.

Nick grinned. "And yours are green like the waters off Maui." He leaned down and kissed her.

His tongue mimicked the motion of his hips. She gasped in sweet agony. The ecstasy of his movements sent spiraling thrills throughout her body. The scent of lime, chocolate and sex filled her head. The curling soft chest hairs tickled her breasts, igniting sparks of pleasure. Involuntary tremors shook her. Her vision blurred as she rose to match his eager response. The intensity of the heat within her took off like a rocket in flight. She went flying beyond the stars into space.

At the same time, Nick stiffened and cried out. Moments later he collapsed on her, burying his face in her neck. Samantha breathed in the scent of him and was filled with a sudden sense of oneness, an incredible completeness.

A while later, cuddled together spoon fashion with the blanket wrapped around them, they stared at the stars.

"I've never done that before."

"Had sex?"

"No, silly. Take control."

"Wow! For a beginner, you're terrific."

Pleased, Samantha smiled and wiggled closer to Nick. "I'll never forget this night."

"You won't, huh?"

"No. I never knew making love could be so…beautiful. So perfect."

"And you were married how long?"

"Almost four years." A lifetime ago, she thought.

"Don't tell me you never made love in all those years?"

"That's not what I'm saying. Edward always took the lead, and we satisfied each other. We may not have been in love, but we were friends and cared about each other. Maybe we were too young to realize what we were missing." She thought for a moment. "I didn't know a woman could…well, feel like this."

He rose on his elbow to look her in the face. "Are you telling me you've never climaxed before?"

"No. I've done that, but never as I did with you."

Samantha caressed his face with her hand.

"Thank you."

"For what?"

"For being the perfect *Stud*." She loved teasing him with Cindy Lou's favorite name.

Nick shook his head. "I told you our first night out. You refused my offer. Remember?"

"Now I know what I've been missing."

An owl flew out of the trees nearby. Nick jumped up and looked around. "We'd better get inside."

"Do you see something?" Samantha checked around, too.

"No. It's safer."

"I've noticed you've been keeping watch."

He nodded and helped her up, before grabbing the blanket and hurrying her inside.

****

The next morning, Samantha lay in bed a little sore, but she'd never felt more alive in her life. Nick's magical hands had worked wonders. He had the right technique to make everything in her build and build until she thought she couldn't live another moment under such pressure. Then, he'd nudged her over the top again and again. She'd shattered with such pleasure she truly saw stars and heard thunder in a cloudless sky. She'd never known how fantastic making love could be or how wonderful one could feel afterward. She wanted to recapture the feeling with Nick—only Nick. How she wished he would have stayed the night with her.

He walked into her bedroom wearing a big grin and carrying two coffee mugs and a box of various kinds of donuts. He handed her one of the cups. "Here's your caffeine fix, sleepyhead."

"My prince charming. Just what I craved." She sipped the coffee and devoured a glazed stick donut. Samantha patted her stomach. "The best breakfast in bed I've ever had."

"You bet." He gave her a quick kiss and gathered up the mugs and the few remaining donuts. "Lounging time is over. Time to move out."

A half hour later, she was dressed and readying the inside for travel. She glanced out the window hoping to see his happy face, only to discover he wore a frown. Did he regret last night?

Once on the road, she knew he was in a snit over something. His grouchy face spoke volumes. She wasn't putting up with his moodiness again. Not after last night.

"Regrets?" There were none for her.

He faced her. "No."

"Then what's the problem?"

He turned back facing the road. "We…ah…played around twice in the same day. That means I wasn't doing my job." Nick looked away. "Do you know what that means to me? I've never neglected my duties. Never."

"I'm sorry. I never looked at it that way. I just wanted to be with you." She touched his arm. "You were alert to our surroundings. I know you were."

"But not as I should've been. Vargas could be released any day. Or suppose his gunmen had found us?" He shook his head.

"But they didn't." Thank you, God.

He ran his fingers through his hair. "We'd both be dead."

"Vargas won't kill me." Samantha glanced down at

her backpack lying at her feet. Tell Nick about the cross. She tried to say the words, but they stuck in her throat. After such a beautiful night, she didn't want to feel his wrath.

"Then why are we running?" He glanced at her.

Samantha shrugged and stared out the window.

He looked at her. "What aren't you telling me?"

Choking on what she really wanted to tell him, Samantha said instead, "What makes you ask that?"

"A feeling since day one."

"If you thought I was holding back on something, why did you make love to me?" Did she really want an answer?

Nick stared straight ahead at the road. "It shouldn't have happened."

"Don't tell me it was a big mistake." *Don't you dare!*

"I'm supposed to *guard* your body, not *use* it." He rubbed the back of his neck.

Use? She didn't feel used. She felt wonderful and wanted to make love again. And again. "You didn't like—"

"Of course I did, dammit." Nick struck the wheel with the palm of his hand. "Don't you get it? I'm supposed to be protecting you."

"Not this again." Samantha grabbed her backpack. "I need to be alone." She got up and moved to her bedroom, slamming the door behind her. Samantha sat on the bed wondering why he had to be all cop. She could understand his need to protect her, but they were safe last night. Vargas could have been near, but he wasn't. They had been taking a chance, but Nick had been aware.

She didn't know how he remembered to keep a look-out under the circumstances. A man like him never lost control, especially when it came to his job. She was sure that bothered him more than anything. The constant struggle he had with himself didn't help either of them. The only way to help him would be to control herself better. That she would do.

The RV slowed. Her gaze went to the nearest window. Nick had pulled over into a rest stop. The vehicle came to a halt. She hurried to the front. "Why are we stopping?"

He turned to face her. "There's a phone just outside. I need to call the captain."

"Speaking of phone calls, I'd like to call my mother in Paris. She'll be worried. I don't know if she's heard about Edward. Your police wouldn't let me call her."

Nick shook his head. "It might lead Vargas to her."

"Oh…my…gosh! You're talking about a hostage." Nick nodded. Samantha tensed. Her mother may not have been Mother-of the-Year, but she was hers.

"Don't worry. Vargas doesn't know where she is or he would have done something by now."

"Thank goodness." Samantha relaxed.

"Stay out of sight. I'll be right outside the door."

"Are…ah…we expecting company?"

"No. But it pays to be careful, something we forgot last night." Nick slipped off his seat and stepped outside.

Samantha knew it was childish and he was right, but she couldn't stop herself from making a face at him behind his back.

****

Moments later with the receiver pressed to his ear, Nick fell against the telephone booth dumbfounded. The thing he dreaded the most had happened.

"I knew of the rumor floating around the precinct, but I hoped they wouldn't release him." Nick ran his fingers through his hair. "I thought the judge locked him up without bail?"

"He has a lot of important people in his pocket, son."

"Dammit." Nick slammed his fist against the telephone booth. He worked his hand to ease the sting of his punch.

"Watch your back. Keep your guard up," Bianco warned.

Last night by the pond would never have happened if he'd known Vargas was on the loose.

"When did he make bail?" He rubbed the back of his neck.

"Two days ago."

"*Two days*?" He let loose with every curse word he knew. "That's when I called. Why didn't you tell me?"

"I found out *after* our conversation. If you'd checked in yesterday, you would have known."

"Yeah. Yeah. It's just not always convenient." Not when he was making out with the D.A.'s star witness.

"Watch yourself. The rumor is Vargas is headed for Texas. He wants Mrs. Thorne with a vengeance now."

"Great. Just what I need. The whole precinct knows I'm camping in an RV. That should help him find us." Nick hesitated before adding, "I didn't know Mike was in your office the other day."

"Mike? He's your partner. We have no secrets

from him."

"Maybe we should." He rubbed his mouth, wishing he could bite back the accusation.

"Is there something I should know, Detective?"

Nick hesitated, not wanting to put suspicion on his partner when he had zilch to back it up. Coincidences, that's all he had. Nothing substantial. "You know Mike. City slicker O'Reilly camping would be a hell of a big joke around the department."

The captain chuckled. "You're right, I'll have a talk with him."

"We may have to make some changes." He pulled on his earlobe.

"Like what?" Bianco's concern evident.

"I'm not sure. Ditching the RV might be a necessity."

"Four more days to trial. Do whatever it takes. Just keep me in the loop."

They said their good-byes and Nick hung up. He stood for a long moment, wondering how he was going to tell this latest bit of news to Sam. She'd been relaxed and happy, trying not to let this whole thing wear her down.

Chico Vargas in Texas meant a whole new ball game.

Chapter 13

Chico Vargas took large strides as he paced his home office. He felt more like himself after washing away the stench of the jail. He brushed lint from the shoulder of his black silk tailor-made suit. Never again would he allow himself to be caged like an animal.

The corner of his lips turned up in a smirk. He knew it would prove beneficial someday to have certain police officials and politicians indebted to him. Now he must find the *woman*, Mrs. Thorne. Chico picked up the letter she sent to him. She possessed the one thing he valued most. The one thing he needed for his family's survival now rested in a thief's hands.

A knock sounded on the door. Chico wished for no interruptions, but he knew his wife of almost a year had come to visit. If she were not carrying his heir, she would be dead. Her ignorance had caused his current dilemma. The loss of the cross and Thorne's subsequent death were the direct results of Maria's carelessness. Now, his freedom was threatened as long as the widow Thorne lived. He would hunt her down like a fox in the woods. He would get his property back before the time of his child's birth. He must. The consequences were unthinkable.

"Enter," Chico shouted, biting his lip to control his temper.

The door opened. A very pregnant, raven haired,

dark-eyed beauty with olive complexion walked toward him. Chico's breath caught in his throat, like it always did when he saw her. He had chosen well. She would produce handsome sons—if she lived. She stepped up to him and kissed him lightly on the lips.

"It is good to have you home, my husband."

"It is good to be home, Maria," he answered in Spanish, the only language he used with her. He motioned for her to sit.

"I'm sorry to have caused you such trouble."

"Not to worry. The heirloom will be mine again." Once the cross was in his possession, Mrs. Thorne would be no more.

"I took the precious cross from the safe only to admire its beauty, my husband. Not to return it to its proper container...I regret much." Maria stared at her hands resting in her lap.

Chico glared at her. If she had left the family gem in its special case, he would never have grabbed it by mistake and taken it to Thorne to be fenced. Holy mother what a thought. To not have the one thing that would save his wife and child was sacrilegious.

"I know the curse, my husband. My life means nothing, but my baby must live. What do you wish for me to do?"

"Take care of my son. I will get the precious cross back." Or die trying. "Rest now." Chico helped her from the chair and to the door.

"Please find it in the heart to forgive me, Chico," she begged, leaving the room.

Never. How could he? His child, his heir, might die because of her stupidity. Damn the curse! Why did his wife and child have to suffer for something that happened decades ago? Why had his family been chosen? All he knew was that many generations ago the Arvalis women were dying along with their first-born sons.

Thanks be to all that was holy, Chico's great, great, great, great grandfather had sought every way possible to save his family's children and extend his lineage. Who would have thought saving a witch's life many decades ago could, in turn, save his baby today?

He wanted to be sure he remembered everything about the spell and how it worked. First, with great foresight, Grandfather had changed their surname from Arvalis to Vargas to protect future generations.

Then a spell was placed on the cross, his family's heirloom. Any wife carrying the heir-apparent in the Arvalis family must have the cross in her physical possession during the delivery of her child. If she did, both mother and child would be spared. If not, they would both die. The magic had worked these many years for his family. And now he, Chico, had lost this valuable heirloom. Chico cursed.

After thirty-six years of wanting an heir, Chico would not let a woman take his dream from him. He would find Mrs. Thorne himself. No more depending on idiots. He would regain his property. Then, he would deal with her.

But he must hurry. His son's birth would arrive soon.

****

Nick pulled into their campsite near Medina Lake a little after three in the afternoon. Once on the campsite they followed a familiar routine. Nick working outside, Samantha inside. She couldn't help but be proud of the accomplishments of two city-slickers-turned-campers.

After dinner and feeling the need to be alone, she had taken a quick shower and locked herself in the bedroom. She had spent the last two hours on her bed in the foulest mood she had been in for some time.

Nick's words, "Vargas could be near," still rang in her head.

The weather just added to her depression. The sudden downpour of heavy rain sounded like small rocks against the tin roof. Even Mother Nature worked against her. A chill ran through her when the strong winds rocked the RV. Lightening clicked and flashed. Not to be outdone, a loud rumble of thunder rolled overhead. Reality could be a bummer.

The fact that Vargas roamed the earth once again put a damper on her whole existence. She had gone numb at the news. A simple breath had become elusive. Nick's concern touched her. She'd spent the entire day putting on a fake cheerful mood in an attempt to convince him Vargas had no effect on her. She hoped he hadn't seen through her charade. The familiar death-grip of fear had returned to strangle her. A mere swallow threatened to bring up dinner.

The object hidden in her face cream must be brought out in the open and discussed. She could only imagine how he would react. Her secret would soon be discovered with Vargas on the loose. Better she told Nick than Vargas, or worse yet, have Nick discover the jewel on his own.

A crash of broken glass sounded outside her bedroom door. Nick cursed.

"Oh, no." Samantha sat up. When she'd taken a shower, she'd left all her stuff on the vanity including the special jar of face cream. She got up and opened the door.

She saw him on his knees in the cramped bathroom holding a gooey piece of jewelry in his hand. She gasped. She knew by the frosty expression on his face he'd never believe any explanation she uttered.

"What's this?" he ordered, his tone frigid.

"I can explain."

"I'll bet." He closed the drain, filled the bathroom sink with water and proceeded to clean the piece of jewelry.

"I'll clean this up." Samantha had to do something to fill the sudden silence. She grabbed some toilet paper and began scooping up the cream.

"Are there more?"

Nick's snarled words made her cringe. She stood up and stepped back into the small hallway. "No. That's the only one." The pulse in her neck throbbed. She cursed herself for not telling him earlier when she'd had several opportunities.

He held up the cross. "What's this bauble worth?"

"I have no idea."

"Is it yours?"

"No." She cleared her throat. "A Vargas heirloom."

"Isn't this a coincidence?" He stared at her with expressionless eyes. "You're hiding something for Vargas right here in our happy home on wheels."

His tone, as cold as dry ice, sent a chill racing through her. His lips thinned and his nostrils flared. Nick's back was ramrod straight. His hands white-knuckled fists. Every breath came faster than the one before.

"I can explain. It isn't like it appears."

He stared at her, his eyes were in slits. "That's what every *crook* says."

His icy words sent a chill up her spine. He put the cross on the counter top and brushed by her, heading for the door.

"I'm not—"

"Tell it to the D. A.," Nick shouted. The RV rocked with the force of the door being slammed shut.

"Please, Nick," Samantha whispered in the silence. She must make him understand. She opened the door and stepped outside into darkness. The major part of the storm had passed. A few large drops of rain felt like golf balls when they struck, but she didn't care. She had to find him. Explain. But his fit of rage had taken him out of sight. A crackle of a branch nearby stopped her. She was out in the open without his protection. Samantha raced back inside the RV.

A sudden loneliness rocked her. Clever Samantha Chadwick-Thorne had managed to alienate the man she loved. Yes, she loved him. She'd known it for sure since they made love. And now he hated her. He believed her to be a *criminal*.

She staggered to the nearby table and sat down. Tears burned her eyes. The word "coward" was a perfect fit for her. Why hadn't she told Nick her secret before this happened? Didn't he save her life several times? Taught her to use a gun? Made things pleasant for her in an unpleasant situation? Why, he even taught her how to survive without a cook and a maid. She had repaid him by keeping things from him.

Samantha hated herself with a passion.

****

Nick leaned against a tree not ten feet from the RV.

Samantha's betrayal made him sick to his stomach. She'd been with him twenty-four seven. They'd laughed. Cried. Even made love together. Yet, she didn't trust him.

He laid his head back, stared into the blackness. He'd been a jerk to hide from her, but he couldn't face her. He didn't trust himself not to strangle her. He should have realized there was a reason she hugged her backpack like a lover. Damn! Why hadn't he searched it? He could kick himself for becoming infatuated with another rich babe and not doing his job.

To think he'd begun to fall for her. A greenback-loaded darling had screwed up his life once before. He'd almost let Sam do the same. At least this time, he wasn't standing at a church altar in front of a couple hundred people. He called himself every name in the book. What in hell was he thinking when he had sex with the state's star witness? Damn. What else could she be hiding from him?

Nick didn't know how long he'd been outside. Long enough for his hot temper to cool and the chill of the dark, damp night to settle in his bones. The curtains were pulled and RV lights were on. At least Samantha remembered some of his teachings.

Conning people was part of his job, but he wasn't a thief or a murderer. Was Sam? Guess it was time to face her and discover the truth before he froze his butt off.

The heat struck Nick in the face when he opened the door. It sure felt good against his chilled hide. Samantha jumped up from the table when he stepped inside. Her red eyes and twisting hands made him feel like a heel.

"You've been gone so long. I was worried."

He waved her off. "I'm a big boy."

"Let me ex—"

"Not now. I'm taking a shower." He needed to warm up. "Make some coffee." Thank the powers that be he'd taught her how. He stepped into the bathroom, closed the door, and came face to face with the cross resting where he'd left it on the counter. Nick groaned. A shot of whiskey sure would taste good now.

****

A lifetime later, Nick emerged from the bathroom wearing a maroon sweatshirt and jeans. The gentle odor of lime filled the room. His dark hair wet and slicked back from his face added to the distrustful frown he wore. Samantha knew when the natural wave dried it would flop over his forehead in a sexy way. Her midsection did a little dance when he grabbed a cup of coffee and sat down across the table from her. She wanted to forget the cross and Vargas. She wanted to take him to bed and make love, but that wouldn't happen.

Nick stared at her. Waited. The truth was all she could give him. If he didn't accept it, she'd be looking out from behind bars. What did she have to lose at this point?

"Where do I start?"

He nodded toward the bathroom. "With your stash."

"It's not mine." He must believe her.

"That gem sure as hell isn't mine."

"Let me start at the beginning."

"Good idea, *Mrs. Thorne*."

The arrogant tone in his voice had been missing for

several days. She deserved anything he handed out, but she missed the softness in his eyes and the sweetness in the tone of his voice. She sighed.

"I told you how Edward had stolen something from Vargas."

"You didn't say you had the sparkler in your face cream."

"Are you going to keep interrupting with your snide remarks?"

Nick leaned back in his seat and crossed his arms in front of him. "Count on it."

Samantha sighed again. *All I can do is tell the truth and hope that he believes me.*

"Tell me. Were you and Vargas partners?"

"How can you say that? He tried to kill me!"

He shrugged. "It could've been a setup."

She looked him in the eye, determined to make him understand. "I am not, nor have I ever been involved with Vargas in any way. Except, of course, to put the man behind bars."

"But you have his expensive bauble in a safe place for him."

"No. I haven't."

"Then it's payment for aiding and abetting a murderer?"

Samantha took a deep breath and let it out. "You haven't believed a word I've said, have you?"

His mouth twisted into a sneer.

She shook her head and continued. "A couple days before Edward was killed, he confessed he had stolen a priceless and very important family heirloom from Vargas. That's all I know. I told you Vargas threatened to kill my mother-in-law and me. Edward thought having the jewel would keep everyone alive."

"You and Edward think alike."

"Using the heirloom to stay alive? Yes, we did. Edward told me to take the cross from the safe and hide it. I did as he requested." She leaned closer to the table. "Vargas discovered the theft and paid Edward a visit. That's what I believe."

Nick bopped his forehead with the palm of his right hand. "That's why you wanted to go to your house."

"Yes. I believed the cross would keep me safe." At that time, she didn't believe Nick could protect her. How wrong could she be? "In a way, I did help to murder my husband. If he'd known where the heirloom was hidden, he'd still be alive." Samantha fought back the tears straining her throat. "Our marriage was doomed and headed for divorce, but he didn't deserve to die."

"Vargas would have killed him anyway." He rubbed his hands over his face. "No thief likes another thief."

"There's something else I didn't tell you."

He dropped his hands and stared at her. She wanted to wither into a ball and roll away. She had to get everything out there once and for all. No way could she look at him while she did. Instead, she watched her nervous hands shake. "I wrote a letter to Vargas. I told him I had the cross, and he would never see it again if he didn't leave me alone." She gulped for air. At last, she'd told him.

Nick jumped out of his seat. *"You what?"*

Samantha jerked back and stared up at him. "Vargas won't kill me before he has his treasure back."

"Let me get this straight." He held out his left hand

and started counting with his right. "You told Vargas you had the cross?"

She nodded.

He moved to the next finger. "You wrote him a letter?"

She nodded again. Not able to look at him, she went back to studying her hands.

Then his middle finger. "You told him you had his precious bauble?"

She hesitated. "Yes."

"This one is hard to believe." He grabbed his index finger and shook it. "You *threatened* him."

When he put it that way, Samantha realized that angering and threatening Vargas made him more determined to find her. How irresponsible could she get? "I'm sorry. I thought I was doing the—"

"Where's the letter now?" The muscles in his face jumping.

"Vargas has it."

Nick closed his eyes and rubbed his forehead. "How long?"

"I mailed the letter the day we rented the RV."

He cursed under his breath and studied her for a moment. "That's what you were doing at the mailbox."

"I was trying to retrieve the letter when you caught me."

"You mailed it"—he thought for a moment— "about seven days ago." He cursed again. "That's how those killers found us so soon."

She cringed.

"Well, that explains that." Nick threw up his hands.

"What?" Samantha frowned.

"Why Vargas is out on bail." His gaze bore into her

eyes.

"You think my letter—"

"Yep. If that piece of jewelry is as important to Vargas as you think, Vargas and his sidekicks are nearby. From now on, we keep moving. We'll stop only to rest. Recess is over."

Their happy times were over, and she had only herself to blame. Why hadn't she told him about the letter before she mailed it? He would have stopped her.

That's why I didn't tell him.

She hugged herself. If only she'd left things up to him. Why hadn't she trusted him back then?

"We're going to have to be on our toes. Both of us."

"I understand." This was her fault. Only hers.

"Do you?" He looked her in the eyes. "I mean no more messing around either."

She straightened her spine. "Yes, Detective."

Nick's brows came together in a deep furrow.

"I'm really sorry about being so ignorant. I'm not very good at this criminal stuff."

"We'll manage."

"One more thing." Samantha smiled when Nick's frown deepened. "It's nothing bad, or at least it hasn't turned out that way."

"Let's have it." He sat back down.

"I brought along a valuable necklace and brooch in case I needed more money."

"And the punch line is…"

"I planned to use them for getaway money and go off on my own," she stated, chin raised.

Nick stared at her, then, busted out laughing. She felt like punching him. "What's so funny?"

"You, on your own? They would have caught you just like that." He snapped his fingers.

"I can take care of myself." She stiffened, backbone straight.

"Need I remind you of the letter?"

Straining to retain her dignity, knowing he was right, she answered, "People learn from their mistakes."

"The dead don't get a second chance."

Nick's words hit home. She slumped back against the seat. "You're right, of course. As a result, Vargas could be in the next campsite." Samantha covered her face with her hands, feeling utterly brainless.

"You were protecting yourself."

"You don't have to be kind. That letter put us in danger." How stupid could she have been?

"Me? Kind? You're kidding, right?"

She touched his arm resting on the table. "You are such a phony. I like you in spite of it." Behind the tough man hid a kind and gentle soul.

Nick stood up. "That's another mistake. Now, get some rest. We're out of here at dawn." He checked the lock on the door before turning to her once again. "First thing tomorrow you're target practicing."

Comfortably warm in their cozy nest, Samantha felt a chill crawl up her back. Would they live through the next four days?

Chapter 14

True to his word, the next morning Nick made a detour to an area sandbank for target practice. Samantha grumbled about the gun, but she was becoming quite the marksman. He chuckled to himself. With any kind of luck, she would never have to face a human target. The thought of someone pointing a gun at her made him want to barf.

He yawned. They'd zigzagged first north toward Austin and then south toward the Gulf. Keeping ahead of a tail was exhausting. Without moving too far east, they'd covered a lot of ground. He'd spent most of the day thinking about the cross and the letter to Vargas.

Stealing, then telling Vargas? Oh, man! Thorne had tried the same trick. What made Sam think she would end up any different? She'd just made herself a bigger target. Sitting next to him, straight and stiff, he could smell her fear though she tried to hide it.

"You okay?"

She turned to look at him. "Of course."

"You look like a sheet of glass about to break." He managed a crooked grin.

"Not really. Just thinking." She twiddled her thumbs.

"Wanna share?"

"My thoughts are not becoming to a lady."

"Ah. But they're the best kind." He wiggled his

eyebrows.

She folded her hands in her lap and turned back to stare out of the window. At least he had gotten a reaction out of her.

"Don't do this to yourself."

"I'm so naïve. Such a featherbrain." She sighed.

"Slow-witted. Dumb. Stupid. Brainless. Obtuse." Nick popped a finger from his fist with each word.

Samantha laughed. "Okay! You made your point."

Nick laughed with her. "That's better."

"I'm sorry I'm such poor company."

"It's done. Now, we figure out what's next."

She turned and touched his arm. "Thanks. I would have been dead by now if it hadn't been for you."

"I don't know. You're one clever lady." He glanced at her and grinned. "All this time I thought you were thinking about how great a lover I am."

"Egotistical. Arrogant. Conceited. Hotshot." She made a fist and popped a finger with each word, mocking him.

"Okay. Okay." He laughed.

"Truth is those…thoughts did cross my mind."

"Gosh-oh-gee. You're going to make me blush." Nick covered his eyes with his fingers spread open. He'd do anything to get her mind off their problems. He needed her to be alert, not wallowing in depression.

"I guess I'm mourning what we had. For a few glorious days, we *were*…a couple. Making love with you…well, it was perfect." She gazed into the distance.

"Worthy of a honeymoon, you think?" *Oh, yeah*!

"Definitely." She turned in her seat to face him.

Nick glanced her way. "You are a responsive and giving partner. There's a lot you bring to a man." He sighed and faced the road once again. "I wish I could be that man, but we're complete opposites."

"Not really." She sniffled.

She fractured his heart. "Look. I live with the slime of this world and you—the filthy rich. That's quite a spread."

"It doesn't have to be." Samantha wiped at her cheek.

"Yeah. It does." He was torn to shreds over knowing how much he'd miss her. Picturing her on the arm of another man, making love—Damn. No more thinking. Life goes on. He would. She would. Nick gave himself a mental shake. He was getting a bit morbid and needed to get off these six wheels for a while. He spotted a convenience store and pulled into the parking lot.

"Why are we stopping?"

"Coffee. Want some?"

"Yes. I'll come with you. It's been a long day sitting."

"Sure has." He got out and went around to help her. "After we get the brew, I'll call the captain." He motioned with his head toward the payphone attached to the store front. They used to be everywhere, but now people were using cell phones. At the time, it seemed like a good idea to leave his home.

"Is there a problem?" Sam looked worried.

"No. Just reporting as ordered." They headed for the store. When they finished paying, Samantha took the coffee and sat in the RV while he made his call.

"Captain Blanco's office, Detective Anderson here."

Nick sobered. Fast. "Mike?"

"Hey partner."

"What in damnation are you doing on Bianco's phone? Nick shook his head and fought to keep his anger under control."

"Only one guy I know who can sing such beautiful music in a man's ear." Mike laughed. "How do you like camping, partner?"

"Knock it off, Mike. Where's Bianco?"

"Living in the outdoors must be the pits. Or maybe the rich widow has you all frustrated?"

"Leave her out of this," he growled. He knew Mike was enjoying himself at his expense. He glanced toward Samantha. "Let me talk to the captain."

"No can do. He stepped out for a minute."

"Why are you answering his phone?" Nick's fingers tightened on the phone. What was Mike up to?

"Don't get your dander up." Mike blew out a breath. "I'm here on orders. The phone rang. I answered it. No big deal!"

"You hate phones." Nick took most of the calls that came in for them rather than listen to Mike bitch.

"Still do."

Nick could picture Mike shrugging in that disjointed way he had.

"I was as surprised as you when I answered it."

"What's happening?" At any other time, Nick would have believed his partner's word as gospel. Right now…he had his doubts.

"Your favorite jewel thief is on the loose."

"Yeah." Nick rubbed his temples. "Any other good news?"

"Scuttlebutt says his nose is pointed toward Texas along with every gunman he owns."

"I heard he might be." Nick turned toward the RV.

"That's the rumor. The man's determined, I'd say." Nick cursed.

"He must have a good idea of your location. Where are you, by the way?"

"Man. That big thing above your lip is at it again." No way in hell would he answer Mike's question.

"Are you talking about my beautiful nose? Remember, I get paid to use it this way."

"If only the taxpayers knew." And what more should we know about you, Mike, Nick thought, watching Samantha sip her coffee.

"I guess you're telling me to mind my own business."

"Now, why would I do that?" Nick hesitated and added, "Tell the captain I'll get back to him."

"Will do. And Nick? Be careful. This guy is after blood."

"Always." Hanging up the receiver, Nick wondered if Mike would be the one to knife him in the back. They had been friends for years, but right now he didn't trust his good friend and partner. Maybe he should talk to Amy Bauer.

"What did Captain Bianco have to say?" Once he sat in the driver's seat, she handed him his coffee.

"It's definite. Vargas is here along with his army." He took a sip of the hot brew and watched the color drain from Samantha's face. "I'd have given anything to keep this from you."

"I need to know everything. We both do. That's how we'll survive this horror." Hand shaking, she sipped her drink.

"You're right." He looked around. "Let's hit the

road. We make a good target out here."

****

Nine o'clock that evening near Corpus Christi, they were still searching for a vacant campsite, but having no luck.

"We should have stopped earlier."

"Yeah." He pulled to the side of the road several miles past the last campground with a "No Vacancy" sign. He shifted into park but didn't turn the motor off. "Settling too early makes us a better target."

"What will we do?" Samantha's brow furrowed.

He thought for a minute. "I saw a mall a few miles back. They sometimes allow RV's to park overnight."

"Can we do that?"

"Unless there's an ordinance prohibiting it."

"How will we know?" She bit her lip.

"If the cops come visiting." Nick turned the RV around and headed back the way they'd come.

"Won't we be too...visible there? At least in a campsite we'd be surrounded by similar vehicles and trees."

"The stores I spotted had a bunch of eighteen-wheelers already parked in the lot. We'll use them for cover."

"What about water? Electricity?" Samantha started tapping her finger on her knee.

"We'll make do with what's in the tanks for tonight. We'd better stock up on supplies while we're there." He needed to figure out a way to get out of sight until the trial.

"We're lucky we carry our beds with us."

"Having this contraption has its advantages." Also, one major disadvantage. The closeness could drive a man crazy.

"Traveling like this isn't that bad, is it?"

Nick glanced over at her, saw the pleading in her eyes. "Not what you're used to, but things could be worse." For a city slicker, he found that he liked camping.

"I'm not the girl I was a few days ago," Samantha said, dead serious.

"No. You're not. You've blossomed on this trip." Had she ever. She kept him in a state of arousal most of the time.

She laughed. "A compliment?"

"Yeah. Just remember I'm still a cop. A con man. A no-good kid from the slums." He regretted the latter two.

"You're a good cop. That kid from the slums no longer exists."

Yeah, he does, Nick thought. More civilized and under control, but there nonetheless. "I'm still a con man."

"Only when it's for a good purpose." Sam's warm smile made his heart crash.

He was in deep, deep trouble!

****

After eating a meal of fries and hot dogs in the RV, Samantha needed some fresh air.

"Can we take a walk or at least sit outside for a while? We've been riding all day, and I'd like to enjoy the evening."

"Sure." Nick grabbed a handful of Tootsie Rolls and stuffed them in his pocket.

Samantha couldn't help smiling to herself. At every store along the way, Nick had replenished his supply of chocolate. "You and your candy. Just the thought of the amount you eat puts ten pounds on my hips."

"Mmm." Nick folded his arms and put a finger to his lips, while he studied Samantha's hips. "They could use a pound or two." Then his gaze wandered to her breasts, the nipples just covered by the green top he'd picked out. "The rest—perfect."

Samantha felt her nipples harden and press against her blouse. No one could have missed her reaction. He didn't. When his eyebrows arched, she could see the desire in his eyes. She could feel his hands touching and caressing her, though he stood three feet away. She felt herself melting and didn't know how much longer her legs would hold her. She wanted to be in his arms.

"Ah...Let's get out of here." Nick's voice was husky.

"You're right, of course." She didn't want him to be. "Will there ever be a time for us?"

He ran his fingers through his short hair. "We have to concentrate on keeping you safe and getting you back for the trial. So, 'til then..." He shook his head.

"You don't have to—"

"Don't get me wrong. I want to explore every part of you and make you forget to think and just feel. I like to watch your heartbeat pulsing in your beautiful soft neck. All those little noises you make when I touch you..." He turned away and added, "If things were different...but they're not."

She could see how talking about what he wanted affected him. She didn't want to beg him, but this question needed to be asked. "When Vargas isn't on our trail, what then?"

Nick looked at her long and hard. "I don't know. I just don't know."

For a moment, she couldn't breathe. She turned away, knowing that her hope for a future with him was slim to none. Sadness filled her. He had too many hang-ups, her money being number one. She felt the pain in her heart but vowed not to let it get her down and ruin the time they did have together.

She stiffened her backbone and raised her chin. "Come on, husband of mine, let's go for that walk."

****

Something woke Nick around six in the morning. He sat up and bumped his head on the ceiling. "Damn. How's a man supposed to move in this crawl space?" he mumbled. Rubbing his bruised head, he jumped out of the bunk. His instincts were screaming at him to get on the road.

A moving target is hard to hit.

He slipped on his pants before he opened Samantha's door. "Sam?"

"What'sa matter?" she mumbled.

"I don't know, but we've got to get going."

Alert now, she sat up clutching the covers to her breasts. "Is Vargas here?"

"Not sure." He tore his gaze away from her breasts. He never got this weird feeling in his gut unless something was about to happen. "I'm going to start driving while you're getting dressed."

"Okay."

"Sit so you don't fall. We'll eat breakfast later."

She nodded. "I'll join you in a minute."

He had the RV back on the interstate heading north in mere seconds. A big SUV went speeding by from the other direction. He recognized the driver. One of the thugs who shot at them. He swore, pressed the gas pedal to the floor and sped down the highway. Quick glances in his mirrors proved Vargas' men hadn't turned around to follow them. Nick gave a sigh of relief. He dropped his speed and turned onto the first side road he spotted. They needed to get off the main highway ASAP.

Once the urgency to disappear had passed, Nick's thoughts wandered back to the vision of sleepy, foggy-eyed Samantha. Those beautiful curls swirling around her head. She looked fresh and childlike with no makeup. Those breasts of hers drew his glance every time. Man. With Vargas on his butt, he worked damn hard at drowning his feelings for her. Seeing the light go out in her eyes about shattered his heart. But he'd done the right thing. They didn't have a chance of having a relationship after she testified. He'd been down that road before with a wealthy woman. His fiancée had ripped his heart out of his chest and done a polka on it. Self-torture wasn't his bag.

"At the speed you were driving, you must have seen Vargas." Samantha stated slipping onto the passenger seat.

"Yeah. A car full of his hoodlums passed us on the road." He glanced at her before turning his attention back to driving. He saw her tense. "Relax. They didn't spot us."

"Thank goodness." She looked outside. "Where are we headed?"

Nick pointed his finger forward. "North."

They rode a while longer before Nick pulled into a shopping plaza and stopped near a payphone. This was another one of those times he wished he hadn't elected to leave his cell phone home. "I want to call Bauer at her home."

"Okay."

"Move to your bedroom and stay out of sight." He nodded toward the back of the RV. "Check the parking lot for familiar faces. If you spot anyone, yell."

She touched his arm. "You're really worried."

"Yeah." The smell of human "skunks" played havoc with his head.

"I trust you *and* your instincts."

He saw the truth in her eyes. Trust meant everything to him. The remaining wall around his heart crashed into a million pieces. He'd waited a long time to have a good woman believe in him. What a hell of a time to find one. Why did she have to be rolling in greenbacks?

"Make your call. I'll be fine." She dropped her hand from his arm.

"Yeah." Nick wanted to grab her and tell her he couldn't stop himself from worrying about her. She'd gotten under his skin. Instead, he opened the door and slipped out of the motor home. He flipped the lock on the door and shut it. He checked around, saw no familiar faces, then picked up the phone.

Amy answered on the first ring. Nick gave a sigh of relief. He didn't want to leave a message on her machine.

"Hi, Am."

"Nick? Is that you?"

"Yeah. I need help. There are too many ears at the precinct."

"What's happened? Did Vargas find you?"

"Have ye no faith?"

She laughed. "Don't ever change."

"I won't. Has anything happened? I tried to get the captain and Mike answered. What's up with that?"

"He told me you got all bent out of shape because he answered the captain's phone."

"He surprised me. Listen, this will be short. I don't want to stay in one place too long. What's the scuttlebutt around the department? Anyone asking questions?"

"You're the main topic of conversation."

"Dammit. I thought I might be."

"Mike keeps asking if anyone knows where you are. But then, he's your partner. He worries about you."

"I suppose." Or was he worried about protecting his own hide? "Anything else?"

"Vargas is rumored to be in Texas."

"I heard that from Mike." He cursed.

"Talk on the street says Vargas wants to make the kill himself. It seems he got a letter from our star witness."

"Yeah. Vargas is probably twitching in his underwear with that one." And so was Nick.

"Very possible. Anyway, that's all I know."

"Thanks, I owe you."

"Just keep Mrs. Thorne and yourself safe."

"I'm working at it."

"Don't trust anyone."

"I never do." And he never would. Nick hung up the receiver and turned toward the RV.

Samantha was waving for him to hurry.

Nick ran back to the RV and jumped in the driver's seat. "What's the matter?" He'd never seen her look this upset.

"Hurry, Nick. Get us out of here. Fast."

"What in hell happened?" He shifted and stepped on the gas.

"H-He's here, Nick." Samantha was bouncing in her seat.

"Vargas? Where?" Nick's gaze shot from one vehicle to another.

"Back there." Samantha waved her trembling hand toward the shopping plaza. "He and a couple men went into a restaurant."

"Oh, sh…crap." They had to do some serious hiding. But where?

Chapter 15

Later that day, Nick grinned and pointed toward an old ramshackle and desperately in need of repair house and barn.

Staring at the structure in front of her, Samantha said, "You've got to be kidding me."

"Never been more serious." Or restless, he thought.

"You want us to stay in that run-down shack?"

"It's perfect," he said, tongue in cheek.

She shuddered. "It's probably swarming with creatures."

"It comes with great camouflage for the motor home." He knew they needed to hide. Their near miss with Vargas and his men that morning was all the proof he needed. They'd followed the Old San Antonio Road east of Austin, past open fields and grazing cattle. Pastureland meant farms. This abandoned farm, partially hidden by trees, was at the end of a long dirt road.

"Oh, gracious." She stared at the lopsided wooden house. "Even a coat of paint wouldn't help this place. All the windows are broken. The door is leaning. We can't stay here."

"All the house needs is a little glass and some elbow grease." Nick bit his tongue to stop from laughing at her. "Now you sound more like the snooty lady I first met."

"Maybe I do. But I'll take my chances. Why, the roof will cave in at the slightest provocation."

"No doubt."

"You do what you want, but I'm staying in the RV." Her chin went up, a sign she wouldn't be budging soon. Nick roared with laughter. She glared at him.

"Let's take a look around." When the RV couldn't be seen from the road, he put his gun in the back of his jeans, turned off the motor and stepped outside. "This is the building that interests me." He nodded toward the barn.

"I can't imagine why. The barn isn't in much better shape than the house."

The lady did have a sense of humor. At least the color had returned to her face. The barn door creaked when he opened it a crack to look inside. The center aisle was open. Everything looked great. Dust floated in the sunrays shining through holes in the roof.

"Reminds me of some of those old westerns on TV. This is where the hired hand would stop the loaded wagon to toss the hay to the second floor."

"How nice. You watch westerns often?"

"Once in a while when I'm in the mood."

"I certainly hope you're not in the 'mood' to play cowboy right now."

"Maybe." Nick looked back at her. She was standing ten feet behind him, uncertainty in her eyes.

"This will do." He pulled the large double door open. It wobbled on its hinges but stayed in one piece. He walked inside, checking the dirt floor for nails or other things that might puncture a tire.

"It smells...barnish in here." Samantha wrinkled her nose.

Nick's brow furrowed. "Barnish? Is that a word?"

"You know what I mean. Old, dusty and animal musty." She sneezed.

"Does it bother your sensitive little nose?" He picked up a rusty pitchfork and rested it against the wall.

"No." She sneezed again. "Yes. You do your thing. I'll be outside."

Nick finished checking out the place and shut the doors. He rounded the corner of the barn in search of Samantha. All he could do was stare at the sight in front of him. She sat in the grass a few feet away, leaning back on her hands, her curly hair only inches from the ground, her eyes closed and facing the sky. He couldn't remember when he'd seen a more beautiful sight. His legs wobbled beneath him, making him grab for the building. She looked like a farmer's daughter in her tight jeans and pale, yellow T-shirt, stealing a few minutes to enjoy the afternoon sun. If only it were true.

Right now, he needed a reality check. He stepped in direct line with the sun. When the shadow crossed Samantha's face, her eyes popped open. Fear came first, then annoyance in those beautiful green eyes. She sat up, and then turned her back to him. "You scared me."

He held out his hand. "We've got to get out of the open."

She ignored his hand and stood on her own. "I've put us in danger again, haven't I?"

"Vargas isn't that close."

"But he could be. Right?"

He wouldn't make it easy for her. She had to be more careful. "You can bet on it," he warned and headed toward the RV.

"Out here," Samantha held her arms out to encompass the area, "the danger seems thousands of miles away."

"Vargas wants us to be confident, to think we're safe. Then he'll pounce. That's why you've been target practicing."

Samantha stopped and touched his arm. "You know I could never kill any living thing, don't you?"

"Yeah. I believe you." At least not willingly, he thought. He looked down at her hand. He could feel the jolt clear to his groin. He laid his hand over hers and looked into her bright eyes. Nick almost drowned in the hopefulness in her eyes. If she kept putting those small well-groomed hands on him and looking at him that way, he'd never be able to keep his distance. He patted her hand and stepped away.

Once in the RV, Nick looked around, checking the area. It was quiet. A farmer worked the land several fields away. "We've been here long enough to draw attention. Let's go."

"You think someone will stop by?"

"Wouldn't you? We'll draw the curious like flies to manure."

Samantha wrinkled her pretty nose again. They got in the camper and headed back to the main road.

"You're really planning to go back there, aren't you?"

"Yep. It's the perfect hideout. But we have to make our moves after dark." Nick headed back toward Austin and the nearest grocery store. "We'll stock up first, then, we'll get a decent meal. It may be the last one we have for a while. We'll be conserving water and eating sandwiches for a few days. We can't risk being seen or do any cooking. I also need to call the captain."

He prayed for the strength to keep his hands to himself and *off her*. They'd have to stay out of sight during the daytime. That meant they'd be confined in close quarters until they flew back to New York. The task ahead of him would be difficult, knowing how he felt about her and what he wanted to do to her. However, they didn't call him iron cop for nothing.

****

They returned to the abandoned farm once darkness fell. Nick switched the lights off just before making the turn onto the driveway. He opened the large front door on the barn, backed the RV in and latched the door once again. If they needed to get out in a hurry, they'd be headed in the right direction. Samantha took the small broom they had purchased and wiped out all the tracks she could see.

They worked together to pull all the curtains to make sure no light could be seen from the outside. They would make good use of the flashlights and batteries they'd purchased earlier that day. Samantha went to her room to get ready for bed. Nick carried a folding lawn chair outside and sat down. He was confident this plan would work, but the conversation with the captain kept churning in his head.

"How are things going, Nick?"

"As good as could be expected."

"Any signs of Vargas?"

"Yeah. But he didn't see us." Thank you, Samantha.

"Good. Good. I'm worried."

"About?"

"Well, now suppose…just suppose mind you, Vargas catches up to you in some hole in the wall hideout. And, God forbid, he kills you."

"Thanks for the trust, Captain." What was he getting at?

"That's not it. Hear me out."

"Go for it." Nick tensed. He didn't like this.

"If the worst happens, and I'm not saying it will, how will I know where to find you? All I know is you're traveling in an RV in Texas."

"Nothing's going to happen to me." Nick clenched his jaw.

"I can name a few widows of cops who would disagree with you. My wife's worried, too. She doesn't like not knowing."

"Tell Mary not to worry. I'm okay." He felt an ache in his chest. She was a second mother to him and he loved her. "Is she still visiting her sister in San Francisco?"

"For another week or so, I guess." The captain's voice cracked. "Can't wait until she's back in my arms."

"Hang in there. You know how women are when they get a chance to visit." Nick felt a tightening in his throat. "I miss her, too."

"I know you do, son."

"You two are family," Nick choked out.

"And you are the son we never had. She'll be home soon," the captain replied, longing in his voice. Bianco cleared his throat. "Getting back to the matter at hand. It's important that I know where you are at all times."

Looking back on the conversation, a sudden wave of guilt hit him. If something did happen to them while hiding in this barn, they might not be found for years. If he could trust anyone in this world, Tony Bianco would be the one. He only hoped the captain's phone wasn't bugged or that someone hadn't been there to hear their conversation.

****

"Something wrong?" Samantha said, standing beside him.

"Just thinking." She startled him, but he would chew his tongue before he let her know.

He stared up at the stars, but he knew exactly what she was wearing—his black plaid flannel shirt over her breast-revealing pink nightgown. His shirt might be large and baggy, but he knew she would be naked underneath that gown. That thought alone alerted a certain part of his anatomy. The sweet, clean fragrance of raspberry body lotion filled the air. He'd recognize it in a field of flowers. He took a deep breath, inhaling the essence of her. Man. How was he going to make it through the next day or two without making love to her again?

"A quarter for your thoughts."

Nick grinned. She was good at throwing his words back at him. He started to get up. "Here, sit in my chair."

She stopped him with her hand on his shoulder. "No. I've been sitting all day. I need to stretch my legs."

"If you're sure?" She nodded and removed her hand. He sat back down and stared off into the blackness of the night. "Funny the tricks life plays on us."

"Yes. They're hilarious at times." She hugged

herself.

"I was living a life from hell when the captain rescued me. I owe him. My life. My freedom. My job."

"You don't give yourself enough credit." She walked to the edge of the barn and looked up at the sky.

"I come from rotten stock. Not the thoroughbred lineage you have."

"It's not what you were, but what you've become that's important."

"Maybe." Nick stared at the distant stars for a moment before continuing, "Wanna know what my old man did when he heard of my mother's cancer?" He didn't give her time to answer. "He skipped town. Haven't seen or heard from him since."

"How did you two survive without the extra income?"

"Ma always worked." He glanced at her. "Me? Stealing." He waited for a reaction, but none came. She surprised him again with her next question.

"He didn't pay her child support?" She turned to look at him, her arms crossed over her chest.

Nick's laugh was short but nasty. "You gotta be kiddin me? Child support? Yep. The back of his hand." He rubbed his cheek. He could still feel the sting.

"What kind of work did he do?"

"My old man never worked a day in his life. He ran scams and conned innocent people out of their life savings." He looked up at her. "That's one trait we have in common."

"You wouldn't do such a thing."

"Cons are part of police work. A con's a con no matter how you look at it." And he was good at working them. He shook his head. "Why in hel…heck am I telling you this stuff? It's done. The past."

"The past is what makes us who we are today."

He wiggled his finger at her. "The shrink is showing."

"Maybe, but we've become friends. Friends talk to each other."

"Just friends?" He looked at her. She was more than a friend to him, but he'd never act on his feelings again.

She leaned against the doorframe, ignoring his question. "You were telling me about you and the captain."

He smiled, remembering. "He caught me stealing a TV set. I wasn't fast enough on my feet."

"You belonged to a *street gang*?"

"No. Just trying to survive." *And help my mother out.*

"It's hard to believe you were a thief, seeing how you are today. Everything about you is all cop."

"Is that a compliment, *Miss Samantha*?" He couldn't see the color of her face in the moonlight, but he'd bet it turned a bright pink. Man. He'd sure miss her.

She smiled. "You know you are, *Detective.*"

"I told you that on day one," he replied, grinning.

"How did that go? Let me think. Oh, yes, I remember. 'I'm good at what I do,' you said back then." She became very serious and continued, "I've learned to trust in what you say, Nick."

Nick leaned forward, elbows on his knees, to cover the overwhelming feeling filling his chest. Best to move on, he thought, before he did something foolish. Again.

"To make a boring story shorter, the captain found

out I was on my own. He and Mary, that's his wife, took me in and became my foster parents. I lived with them until I graduated from the police academy."

"You have great respect for him, don't you?" She stepped back to lean against the barn.

"He's the best. Mary is, too." His voice softened. Besides his mother, Mary and Bianco were the only other two people he had ever loved.

"They must be proud of what you've become."

"Some of the time, maybe." He squirmed in his chair.

"I'd guess all of the time. You've done well."

Nick glanced back at Samantha. She smiled at him. Receiving praise of any sort always made him nervous. "Thanks for listening." He leaned back. God, she was beautiful standing there with the moonlight glistening on her hair, her face aglow from its recent scrubbing. What he wouldn't give to be able to take her into the nearby field, rip his shirt off her and make love to her with only the moon and the stars as witnesses. Oh. Hell. He got up and folded his chair.

"Come on. Let's try to get a good night's sleep." He didn't know how he'd accomplish it with her close and naked under her gown, but he'd have to try. "We never know what tomorrow will bring."

"Let's hope we have a wonderful day." She turned to go inside.

"Sam?" He arched a brow. "Lock your door tonight."

Chapter 16

Samantha tossed and turned all night. It was after 9:30 by the time the silence woke her. Had Nick left her? She slipped on the yellow top and jeans she'd worn yesterday. She opened her bedroom door and gave a sigh of relief. Nick was sitting in the driver's seat, staring out the front window. The driveway was visible between the cracks in the barn.

"Hi. Sorry I overslept. I didn't realize how tired I was." She walked to the front seat and yawned.

"Not much else to do." Nick raised his arms above his head, stretching.

"Anything moving out there today?"

"Traffic. A hungry cow." He pointed to one munching on grass over by the fence.

"How's the weather?" Something was bothering Nick.

"Sunny. Hot."

"What's wrong?" She'd had enough of the small talk and his short answers.

"Not sure." He pushed his fingers through his already disheveled hair. "Things look quiet." He shook his head.

"Do you think Vargas knows where we are?"

"That's the sixty-four-thousand-dollar question."

"Maybe we should leave." Samantha sat in the passenger seat to peer out through the cracks in the barn door.

"We've only got one more night. Captain told me the D.A. wants you in Albany by two." He yawned. "Tomorrow, we'll catch the early flight out of Austin."

"I'll be glad to get Vargas convicted and get back to normal." Whatever that is, she thought. No Edward. No Nick. Just an empty, quiet house. She choked back her tears.

"You okay?"

"Just wondering what life will be like when this is over."

He returned his gaze to the driveway before saying, "You'll go back to your social clubs, your teas and rich friends."

"Who was she?" Samantha knew there was someone. "The woman who broke your heart."

"Iron hearts don't break."

"Yours is as soft as a marshmallow." When he snorted, she continued, "She's wealthy, isn't she?"

Nick turned to face her, his eyes blank. No expression whatsoever. Then he began to shake his head.

"I'd like to know." She needed to understand him.

"Filling your head with crap again?"

"Knowing about you isn't 'crap' of any kind."

"Haven't learned much on this trip, have you?" His lips tightened across his teeth while his blank stare focused over her shoulder. Silence thickened the air. "Her name is Joanne. A note arrived at the altar instead of a bride."

"I'm sorry." Samantha wanted to give him the hug he needed. His hands-off attitude forbade it.

"Don't be." He looked her in the eye. "I learned a

valuable lesson."

"What did the note say?"

"She'd eloped with her ex-beau. Her *wealthy* ex-beau."

"No wonder you've been tossing out remarks about rich snobs." She wanted to touch him, to comfort him, to assure him that she wouldn't leave him. Anger at Joanne filled her. Nick had lost another person he loved.

"Oh, yeah. I forgot." He leaned toward her to make his point. "Jo decided she couldn't live on a '*poor cop's salary*'."

"Oh…" She touched his leg. "I didn't know."

He motioned between the two of them. "Now you understand why a relationship wouldn't work between the two of us."

"I'm not like her." She loved him. She'd cling like glue.

"Tell me about it. Didn't you marry a man with money?"

"Yes. But—"

"The evidence is in. Case closed." He turned his seat to the front, causing her hand to slide off his leg.

The sudden loss of his warmth made her want to grab his leg and pull him back. Instead, she sat there, simmering. What could she say to a man who thought wealthy women were gold diggers and status seekers? It was no wonder he'd passed out all those sarcastic remarks on this trip. He'd find out Samantha Chadwick was nothing like Joanne. "Well, Detective, I'm reopening the case."

"It's sealed."

"I'm unsealing it!" Samantha stared at him until

Nick glanced back at her with a deep-set scowl on his face, his teeth clenched. "Yes, I knew Edward had money, and we now know where it came from. Yes. I married him, but not for love, money, or social status. I married him to spite my parents.

"I'm not proud that I used Edward in that way. At the time, I thought I was doing the right thing. Believe me when I say I paid a high price for that rebellion. I'm still paying." She took a deep breath. "If you take note, *Detective*, you will see my situation is the complete opposite from Joanne's."

"When it came time for a stroll down the aisle into the arms of a lowly poor cop, you'd run as fast as those gorgeous legs could carry you. Just like Joanne did."

Samantha felt Nick's burning gaze traveling from her toes to the top of her head and down again. It didn't resemble the warm and tender looks he had given her in the past. It did nothing to encourage her. He was saying good-bye. She wanted to weep. However, his next words made her angry.

"You're not bad on the eyes, but when we're back in the real world, you'll soon forget our little excursion into fantasy land."

The force of his words hurt her to the core. He really didn't think very highly of her. How could she love such a cold man? The more she thought about his words, the more her anger boiled. She jammed her hands on her hips. "You arrogant jerk!"

He raised his hands as if to ward off a blow. "Now, Sam."

"Don't you 'Now Sam' me, you hypocrite. I'm not the snob. You are. You're the one looking down your nose at me. Money doesn't make a person. It's what's in here"—she pressed her hand to her heart—"that counts. You're right. You do have a heart of iron." She got up and reached for the door. Nick grabbed her arm. She turned around and glared at him. "Take. Your. Hands. Off. Me."

"Shut up and sit down."

"Why you bully. You…"

Nick pointed to the driveway. "A black SUV is coming."

In an instant, all else slipped away. Her fear returned. She peered out the front window while a lively worm did a fast crawl up her spine once again. She shivered. "W-who is it?"

"Can't tell. It looks like one person."

"What do we do?"

"Sit tight. Let's see who it is." Nick drew his gun, checked it for ammunition, and then returned his gaze to the approaching car.

Sit tight? Samantha wanted to make that run to the back forty. Instead, she sat staring out the window, hoping that Nick couldn't see her shaking. The gentle squeeze of his hand on her shoulder told her differently.

****

For Samantha's sake, Nick hoped their visitor was a local checking on the property. She'd been through enough and didn't need to be scared spitless by some paid assassin. Tomorrow couldn't come fast enough. Then his job would be done. And just in time. Before he did something stupid again.

Nick stared hard at the figure in the car. Captain? Naw. Couldn't be him. He's in New York. The car stopped several feet in front of the barn. The driver sat for a moment before opening the door and stepping out.

"I'll be damned. It is Bianco." What in hell was he doing here? Every warning signal he relied on came to full alert, sounding a massive alarm in his head.

"That's great. Right?" Samantha leaned back in her seat.

"Maybe." Maybe not.

"He's one of the good guys, isn't he?"

"Yeah. You stay here and keep out of sight." When she started to argue, he raised his hand to stop her. "Let's not blow it now."

"Okay." She stood up and turned toward the kitchen. "But you be careful."

Nick smiled at her. "I'm always careful. Now scoot." He tapped her rear to hurry her along to the back of the RV. She glared over her shoulder at him. "And Sam? Get your gun."

The fact she didn't argue told him how upset she was. He waited for her to disappear from sight before he left the motor home, making sure to lock the door behind him.

Was Mary okay? Tony never followed his men on a case, and definitely not across the country. Nick and people like him did the fieldwork, reporting back to their leader. He rubbed his stomach. His gut was churning. What in hell was going on here?

"Nick? Is that you in there?" Captain Bianco yelled. "Come out here where we can talk."

Nick tucked his gun into his waistband before opening the barn door and stepping outside. He met the captain halfway and shook hands.

"It's good to see you, son."

"Same here." Nick glanced over at the SUV, but it was too far away to see inside. "You're a long way from Kirkland County."

"Well, I wanted…" Bianco looked back at the car and then at the barn before his gaze returned to Nick. "Ah…Where's Mrs. Thorne?"

"What's up?" Nick had never seen Bianco this nervous. The man was twitching in his shoes. He was standing in front of the man he trusted with his life, yet his own stomach was doing flips. Nick's gaze wandered the fields around the barn before settling on the SUV. Not a soul in sight, but his gut instinct screamed at him to be careful. But this was his friend, his mentor.

"I'm here to make sure Mrs. Thorne gets home safe."

"You don't trust me to do my job?" The hair on the back of his neck not only stood up but felt like it did a constant jig.

"Of course I do."

Nick looked past the captain at the vehicle. He thought he'd seen a brief flash in the SUV. He needed to get closer to get a better look. He moved toward the SUV. Bianco caught him by the arm.

"Where are you going?"

"Just being cautious."

"There's nothing to be concerned about. Bring Mrs. Thorne out here, and we'll get out of this heat."

Nick studied the man's face. Nervous, yes, but why was he seeing fear in his eyes? That's when he knew someone was in the SUV. Someone was holding his captain at gunpoint. Nick lowered his voice. "Who's in the SUV?"

Bianco's gaze moved from Nick to the SUV to Nick.

"Vargas?" Nick whispered.

When Bianco's head nodded ever so slightly, Nick knew he had a fight on his hands.

Why had Bianco brought Vargas right to his doorstep? One thought kept reeling in his head. Had the most honest man he knew in this world, the one he loved and trusted with his life, turned crooked?

"Just get the woman and everything will be okay."

"You trained me better than that, Captain."

"I know, but…"

"Ah, but the trainer is not so good at following his own rules," Vargas commented in broken English, opening the SUV's door and stepping out with gun in hand. Two men followed him, aiming guns at Nick.

Nick's gaze flew to the Bianco's. "You're the mole?" Not Mike like he thought?

"Great job, Captain. You fooled the great detective. We worked together to find my cross and Mrs. Thorne."

"Tony?" Nick couldn't believe his own ears.

"I'm sorry, son. Mary—"

"Mary doesn't know about you and Vargas, does she?"

Bianco shook his head. "But Mary—"

"Mary would hate you for this." Nick couldn't believe the man who had taught him to love and obey the law had turned against it. Had become a crooked cop. He wanted to puke.

"*Si'*. Everyman has a soft spot, even you, detective."

"I don't have *a soft spot*, slime ball." At the moment Nick hated this man with a passion.

"Oh, I forgot. You are made of steel."

"Iron. That's the rep."

Vargas's smile faded and his face turned ugly. His lip curled. His eyes blazed with fierce hatred. Nick wanted to step back, but he held his ground. No crook would get the best of him as long as he could breathe.

"Enough! No more sentiment. Get the woman."

Bianco turned toward Vargas. "You promised to let me handle this."

Vargas waved away his comment and snarled, "Get the woman," to one of his men. The man headed toward the barn.

"What woman?" Nick tried to stall. The gunman stopped.

"Do not play dumb with me. She has my property. I need it back. Pronto!"

"And what would that be?"

"A cross."

"Oh, yes. That little bauble you murdered a defenseless man to get?"

"I will do it again. I need the cross to save my son." Vargas motioned for his man to get moving.

"I don't think so." Save his son? What in hell was he talking about? Nick spread his legs, ready to fight.

"Don't get yourself killed over this," Bianco pleaded, keeping his gaze on Vargas. "Mary would never forgive me."

"Sorry. No can do."

"Then you die." Vargas raised his weapon.

The other gunman stepped next to Vargas. "You want me to pop him, boss?"

"No. The woman, now." Vargas motioned with his arm to the man who had taken a stepped toward the barn.

Nick gave a silent sigh of relief. At least he'd live a

few minutes longer.

Vargas smiled at Nick. "I've looked forward to this for a long time. You are slippery like a fish. This pleases me."

"Life is tough."

"Yes. It is so." Vargas aimed his weapon at Nick.

****

Samantha, unable to stay hidden in the bedroom any longer, peeked out the front window just as Vargas pointed his gun at Nick.

He's going to kill him.

"Damn you, Vargas." Samantha muttered, gun in hand and determined to stop him anyway she could. She hurried out the back door of the barn. Staying close to the building, she made her way to the front, where she could see Nick. Samantha took several deep breaths and prayed for help. Her hands were trembling. Her heart was beating double time. God, she was scared. Now or never, she thought.

Before she could make her move, Vargas fired his gun. Bianco jumped in front of Nick. They both fell to the ground, motionless. Vargas moved closer and aimed his gun at Nick's head.

Without thinking of how she was exposing herself, Samantha yelled, "Vargas." Suddenly, three guns were pointed at her. But she held Vargas steady in her sights, clasping the gun with both hands the way she'd been instructed. Her legs were spread to steady herself. All signs of nervousness were gone. She had never felt calmer in her life. Vargas had taken her love away from her and he would pay. She needed to do this for Nick. Vargas would not live another minute.

He grinned at her. "At last we meet. You have

made quite the chase, Mrs. Thorne."

"And you're dead." Samantha held the gun steady and fired. The stunned look on Vargas' face before he fell gave her great pleasure. "That's for Nick, you piece of scum."

The two gunmen, shocked to see their boss fall dead to the ground, hesitated. Samantha, overcome by the thought of Nick's death, dropped her gun and crumpled to the ground.

Two more shots rang out. Two men fell like pins in a bowling alley.

Then there was silence.

****

"Sam? Dammit, Sam, where are you shot?" Nick knelt next to her, checking her body for blood.

"Nick?" Samantha bolted upright, wrapping her arms around him. "I thought you were dead."

He shook his head. "Not again?'

"But I saw Vargas shoot you."

"Not me. You okay?" he insisted. She nodded. "Then I'll see to the captain." He picked up her gun, tucked it behind him in the small of his back and ran to Tony.

She followed close behind, stunned to see that Vargas and his goons were dead.

I killed Vargas. She shivered. Her stomach churned at the sight of all the blood.

"Is Captain Bianco alive?" Samantha hugged herself, thankful she hadn't eaten breakfast.

"Yes. A shoulder wound." Nick tossed the captain's cell phone at her. "Call nine-one-one. Hurry."

Chapter 17

The job. That's all Nick had left. He hadn't seen Sam since the local police escorted her back to New York. She had shot Vargas and killed him with one shot. Damn. He couldn't be prouder. He'd forced himself to let her go. She deserved better than he could give her.

What a hell of long two weeks he'd put in since his world crumbled. Nick still found it hard to believe the man he respected was a crooked cop. In just a few minutes, he'd finally face Tony Bianco for the first time since returning home. Nick tasted the bitter bile creeping up his throat as he entered the cellblock that housed his mentor and longtime friend. He would rather be headed for death row himself than to see Tony locked up.

Nick rounded the final corner. There stood Tony, his mentor, behind iron bars. A place he'd sent many criminals. A knife-like feeling twisted in his gut.

"Good to see you, Detective." Tony's eyes brightened for a moment, then darkened as if someone had turned off an internal light.

Unable to speak, Nick nodded. He fought the urge to run. He couldn't stop staring at the man in front of him. This slump-shouldered, shriveled man, with the sunken cheeks and sad eyes, couldn't be the proud, tall authoritative sparkling-eyed giant he had admired all these years. Nick locked his knees in a wide stance, crossed his arms over his chest.

Tony cleared his throat. "I'd offer you a chair, but—"

"Why?" Nick's voice cracked, interrupting him. "Why did you do it?" Nick stepped toward the cell.

Tony stepped up to the bars and whispered, "For Mary."

Nick's anger jumped up a notch. "Damn you!" Nick shouted through clenched teeth. Instant fury choked him. He stiffened and took a step closer to the bars. He grabbed the bars and shook them, wanting to strangle the man in front of him. Mary was a great lady. She would never want him to join the likes of Vargas. Never. "Don't put this on her."

"I'm not." Tears filled Tony's eyes.

"You? *A crooked cop?*" Utter disgust boiled up and spilled over in two words he never dreamed he would be saying to his captain.

"Son—"

Nick tightened his white-knuckled grip on the bars. "You. Are. No. Father. To. Me." He said, shouting every word. "Not anymore."

"You will always be a son to me." Tony lowered his head, deflated.

Nick hadn't missed the terrible sadness in his mentor's eyes. He cursed under his breath, yanked his hands off the bars and turned away. Guilt filled him. He'd never spoken to Tony that way before. Seeing Tony like this tore him apart. Anger rose in him like a fire in an elevator shaft. He wanted to scream. Why Tony? He wanted to rip out those bars and free his friend. He wanted to turn back time and reverse

Bianco's decision to spy for Vargas. He wanted the only father he'd really known to be the man he thought him to be—a good, honest, kind-hearted cop.

But things had happened. They couldn't be changed.

And it hurt. God. How it hurt.

"Nick?" Nick refused to look at him. "The truth is I lied to you."

He jerked around, saying, "You did what?" Renewed rage shot through him. Wasn't it enough he had set him up? Now he admits he'd lied. Tony had always been honest about everything, a trait Nick admired.

"Mary wasn't visiting her sister or anyone else."

"But, you told—"

"I know what I said." Tony grabbed the bars with both hands. "But everything was a lie."

"You never lied to me." Nick shook his head, trying to understand what Tony was saying.

Tony raised his hands to calm Nick. *"Vargas had her."*

"What?" Nick stared at his mentor and wondered what demon had temporarily possessed Tony's body.

"Vargas had her in some damp, cold hole as a hostage. He used her to get to me. And thus, to Mrs. Thorne." Tony rubbed his hand over his face. "I was so scared he would kill her." His chin quivered. "What would I have done without my Mary? She's my life."

"Oh. Hell." Nick didn't know what to say. That slime bucket had his filthy hands on Mary? His breath became ragged, his fear building. He didn't know if he wanted to know the rest, but couldn't stop himself from asking, "Where is she now? Is she okay?"

"Home. When his gunmen learned Vargas was dead, they set Mary free. I'm just grateful she's unharmed." Tony sobbed. Nick hated watching Tony's strong face crumple in such agony. Mary was safe at home. She'd never gone to San Francisco. Instead, she'd been kidnapped?

"I haven't heard a peep out of anyone about Mary's disappearance."

"That's because I've asked a favor of the D.A. and my lawyer to save it for my trial. I don't want Mary to face the embarrassment of the press right now." Tony leaned against the bars.

That's the first thing that made sense to Nick. Tony would protect Mary against all adversaries. He would, too. Nick ran his fingers through his already tussled hair and blew out a long breath.

"I'm damn glad she's okay." Relief warmed him. He'd be sure to stop by to see Mary when he left here. Nick cursed Vargas's parentage. "You should have told me. We could have worked this out, and you wouldn't be in jail."

"I did my best to keep you out of it." Tony rubbed the back of his hand under his nose.

"Then why did you leave me ignorant of the facts and in the middle of this mess?"

"I knew you would protect Mrs. Thorne. You are the best." Tony shrugged his shoulders. "I also figured I could protect you in return. After the first couple nights, I purposely didn't want to know where you were hiding Mrs. Thorne. Then Vargas threatened to shoot Mary in her beautiful face with a shotgun." Tony rubbed the back of his neck. "I couldn't let that happen."

"You took a bullet meant for me." Nick glanced at

Tony's shoulder.

"I'd do it again in a heartbeat."

The love he saw in Tony's eyes reflected what he felt in his own heart. Nick's anger drifted away. How could he not forgive this man who loved him and would have died for him? A man who worshipped his wife so much he had forfeited his lifetime career. That was pretty heavy stuff.

He cleared his throat to ward off the emotion choking him. "I tried to see Mary several different times. Why did she refused to see me?" That hurt. Mary was a mother to him.

"Mary made herself unavailable to you because she wanted me to tell you everything. She knew you'd eventually come to me." A grinned cracked at the corner of his lips. "It just took longer than we thought."

"And she's okay with," he motioned to the cell, "all this?"

"She is. We've done a lot of talking since I've been here. Though she thought I should have had you help me find her, she understands why I didn't."

All this emotional stuff was choking Nick. "I hope I find a woman like Mary someday."

I had her and let her go.

"You've already found her, son. She loves you."

Nick's gaze snapped to Tony's. "You've seen her?"

"She came to see me a week ago." Tony chuckled. "Can you beat it? She actually thanked me for saving your life."

Nick wanted to go to her, capture her in his arms and never release her. But he couldn't. "I'm not worthy of her, Tony."

"The hell you're not." Tony yelled. "You're a fine man. The best."

"Nah. I'm a con artist like that deadbeat who sired me. It's in the genes." How he wished otherwise.

"You're nothing like him." Tony held up his hand and stressed his point one finger at a time. "You're a decent law-abiding man. You do your job and do it well. You set murderers up for arrest. Your reward is the satisfaction of putting crooks behind bars. And most important, you make no profit."

Nick studied his foster father. Then he smiled. Even locked behind bars, the man could still set him straight.

Tony's voice softened, "You love her?" Nick shrugged. "Answer me, boy."

Nick grinned again. At thirty-four, Tony still called him a boy and had done so since he was fourteen. "Yeah. But—"

"No buts about it. True love comes once in your life. I know this for a fact." Tony's voice grew stronger with each word like it always did when he scolded Nick. His stature straightened. "Don't blow it because some ditzy, rich broad didn't know what a good man she had."

"Okay. Okay. I'll think about it."

"You've already done the brain work. Now go get her." Tony waved him away.

He felt a weight lift from his chest. Suddenly he felt much lighter. More relaxed. Happy. Only his friend could have said the words that would make him go after the one woman who had become his world. "Thanks…Dad."

"That's the first time you've called me that."

Tony's eyes swam in moisture.

"Get used to it, Dad." Nick stepped to the bars and pulled Tony into a bear hug. They stood locked together for a long time.

When they separated, Tony wiped his eyes on his shirtsleeve. "Enough of this bull. Stop spending time with this old goat and go get your future."

"You're my future, too. Don't ever forget it." Regardless of the way Tony saw his future, Nick still doubted he and Samantha could make it together. He'd have to think about it.

****

Sitting in her oversized chair in the living room, Samantha realized she finally had the one thing she desired all her adult life—freedom. She could make her own choices, buy and eat junk foods if it suited her, wear jeans and lounge around all day and ignore invitations to teas and other social events. It was all within her grasp, but she craved something more. How immature and ungrateful could she get? The one person she needed most of all was missing.

Nick O'Reilly.

She'd made many changes in her life during the last weeks. It hadn't been easy. She'd wandered her lonely Victorian mansion wallowing in self-pity for a couple days. Then she'd straightened her Chadwick backbone and gone to work. True love conquers all, they claim. It's obvious *they* never ran into a blockhead named Nicholas O'Reilly. She was irrevocably in love with a man who couldn't get past his own background and her wealth.

She missed him.

She needed him.

She loved him.

It hurt. It hurt a lot.

"Enough of these depressing thoughts." She'd wash away her troubles in a good hot bubble bath. She headed for the stairs. The doorbell rang. "Now who could that be?" When she opened the door, she hung tight to the knob or she would've collapsed. There stood the man of her dreams, looking exactly like the day she had first met him—black leather jacket, faded jeans, T-shirt, and well-worn boots and still in need of that motorcycle. He looked delicious. Just the food her hungry eyes needed.

"Hi, Sam."

"I have plans, Detective. Is there something you wanted?" She surprised herself with that statement.

"Is that any way to greet an old friend?" He grinned from ear to ear.

Oh, he wouldn't get off that easily. "Why are you here?" It had taken him four weeks to come to her. Now, it was her turn to make him suffer a little.

"Hey! You're wearing the jeans I picked out. You like them?"

His gaze took in everything about her. She fought the shiver trying to rack her. She had missed that telling look. The one that let her know he wanted to grab her and ravish every inch of her. "I've gotten used to them. What do you want?"

She still clutched the door, making sure he couldn't walk past her. Hang on the door or jump into his arms. Those were her choices. She couldn't do the latter. Not yet.

"Sorry, I haven't been around. I...ah...had things to settle."

"Things? Such as?" Keeping her expression noncommittal was difficult.

"You're not going to make this easy for me, are you?"

He ran his fingers through his hair in the way he did when he was nervous or under pressure. She wanted to laugh but held back. She enjoyed watching him struggle. It brought out a new side of Nick she hadn't seen.

"If that's what you came to say, then good day, Detective." She stepped back and shut the door. Nick jammed his foot over the threshold at the same time. Not expecting his reaction, the door bounced back, just missing her.

"Ouch! Are you trying to cripple me?" Nick moaned and arched his brow.

"I wish." She continued to hold the door against his foot. At that moment, she wanted to ring his big handsome neck. He could be very frustrating at times. She just wanted him to get to the point and make love to her. But, darn. She would control this situation for a while longer.

****

One look at Samantha made Nick wonder why it had taken him another two weeks after talking to Tony to knock on her door. He still believed he wasn't good enough for her, but there he stood in front of her, grinning like a love-struck idiot.

She was more beautiful than he remembered in the sexy green blouse and blue jeans he had bought for her. Inhaling the fresh flower scent about her made his head spin. How he loved this woman. He needed her more than air to breathe. But would she have him?

Nick frowned. Maybe she didn't love him. Could Tony have been wrong? She sure didn't act like a woman welcoming her man home. Sam looked more like she could string him upside down from her favorite tree and laugh at him while the blood rushed to his head, killing him slowly.

"Come on, Sam. Let me in. We need to talk."

She studied him for several seconds, then let the door go and headed for the kitchen. "You've got five minutes." She looked at her jeweled watch. "Starting now."

"I thought you rich types were trained to be more sociable." He cursed and wished he could take back his words.

She glanced at the time. "Four and a half minutes."

"Hey! We're in the kitchen, and it's a beauty."

"I'm glad you can recognize that."

Nick looked around. Wow, he thought. Lots of windows and room to spare, making it a cheery place to hang out. The cream-colored walls, walnut cabinets with appliances to match, a small table with comfy chairs—it reminded him of the kitchen he and his mother had dreamed of having one day. They hadn't thought of a huge chandelier of the type hanging in the center of the room, but it was a nice touch. He liked the way it opened to a bright dining room loaded with more windows. If only Mom could see this...

"But I thought your cook ruled the kitchen. By the way, where is she?" Nick checked out an open doorway.

"Things have changed."

"You fired her?"

"Of course not. She's on an extended holiday."

"You must be ordering out a lot." She certainly couldn't be preparing her own meals, could she?

"No." She glared down her nose at him. "I'm taking cooking lessons."

Nick smiled. "Good girl. But I was your first teacher."

Samantha arched a brow, looked at her watch. "Four minutes."

"Okay. Okay. Can a thirsty man have a drink?" This wasn't working out like he planned.

Samantha marched to the refrigerator, grabbed a can of root beer, and tossed it to him.

"Jeesh. Now it's going to foam all over your spotless floor," he teased.

She checked the time once again. "Three minutes."

"Man, you're tough. I don't think I remember you being so hard on a guy." He opened the soda over the sink and watched the foam run down the side as predicted.

"Two minutes."

Nick took a sip of the soda and took his sweet time getting to the reason he came. A quirky side of him wondered what she would do at the end of the five minutes. He smiled to himself. She wouldn't be kicking him out. He was here to stay—forever.

"One minute."

"Have a heart, Sam. Pressure makes me stutter."

Samantha put her hands on her hips. "Ha! You never stuttered a day in your life."

"Well, now. How do you know that?" He'd forgotten just how much he enjoyed the bantering between them.

"Zero minutes." She marched to the back door and

opened it. "Good day, Detective O'Reilly. Don't bother to come back."

If he took her up on her offer, what would she do? He meandered over to the kitchen chair, turned the back to face her and straddled it. "You'd better close the door. It's getting cold in here." Undeterred, he guzzled his soda.

She slammed the door. "Fine." She grabbed the telephone hanging on the wall.

He was out of his chair and yanking the wire disconnecting the phone before she could bring it to her ear. His reason for being there did not include his leaving without her. The sooner she realized that the better things would go between them.

"Smooth, Detective. What's your next move?"

"Be patient. We need to talk."

"I don't think so."

"Well, I do."

When he held out his hand to her, she quickly moved to sit on the opposite side of the table. That made him frown again. He didn't like the way she was acting. Not at all. If he didn't get this woman in his arms soon and say what he had to say, he still might get his backside booted out of there. He couldn't let that happen.

****

Samantha sat tapping her fingers on the table. When would this man get to the point? True, she made things hard for him, but that never stopped him before.

"I heard you're selling Edward's business."

Surprised he knew, she nodded. "What good is it to me? I'm not a jeweler."

"Someone could run it for you."

"And have another person like Vargas come along and threaten me? No thank you."

"A little bird told me you plan to become a CEO, too."

She put her finger on her lips and thought for a moment. "Oh. Yes. I remember. Being a CEO interferes with me attending all those social clubs and teas with my rich friends."

Nick grabbed his chest with his hands. "Oooo. A direct stab to the heart."

Samantha lifted her chin. She got him on that one.

"No kidding, Sam. I like what I've heard."

"Just what have you heard?" She leaned forward, anxious to hear what he knew about her plans.

He smiled. "Really?" She nodded. "Let's see. You might have a buyer for the store and the box of jewelry you keep in the safe."

"Wow. You know about the jewels." That surprised her. "What else do you know?"

"You have started the paperwork to start your own business. A business that will help my friend Joey get a home to live in instead of a tent. I'm glad you've figured out a way to make my buddy's life easier."

"Once everything is final, the first thing the New Start Foundation will do is provide a nice home for Joey and his mother." That's one thing she can't wait to accomplish. She will rest easier knowing Joey was living in a safe environment.

"Thank you. At least he will know we hadn't forgotten him." He smiled. "I miss the kid." His voice cracked. He cleared his throat. "The New Start Foundation is a great name, a great idea. I know you'll be a top-notch administrator. I'm impressed."

"New Start isn't being founded to impress you or anyone else. My intent is to help Joey and other children in bad situations."

"I know. You're a kind, giving woman with a big heart. Something of this type has been needed for a long time, and you're the perfect person to make it successful."

Samantha's gaze shot to Nick's. "Thank you. I'm glad you approve." This man, who always sneered at wealth and all it stood for, really did think highly of her and her ideas for the Foundation. Oh, how she loved him. "At least Edward's dirty money and fenced jewels will be put to good use making children happy."

He nodded in agreement. "Speaking of kids, what did you think of the cross's secret?"

"You mean the curse on mother and child?"

"Yeah. All this time we thought Vargas wanted the cross back for the money value." He shrugged.

"Instead, Vargas needed the cross to protect his wife and unborn child. At least he valued life in some way." Samantha crossed her legs. "Do you think the cross really could protect mother and child during delivery?"

"The important thing is that Vargas and his wife believed it." Nick chugged the rest of his soda and set the can down on the table. "When Mrs. Vargas came to the precinct and explained the situation, not a single cop questioned her story. They were happy to give her the cross and wished her well."

"Cursed or not, she and her newborn son are alive and healthy." Samantha wished she had a son. Nick's son.

"In my opinion, they're both better off without

Vargas. The man was rotten to the core except when it came to his kid."

"I guess that was his one and only redeeming feature." She cleared her throat. Why didn't he get to the reason why he came? "How's the captain? Have you seen him since you got back?" She couldn't imagine how difficult it must be for Nick to see the man he worshipped and trusted above all others behind bars.

"That's one of the things I wanted to talk about."

Samantha stared at him without saying a word.

"The toughest thing I ever did was to see him in jail." Nick stood up and began to pace. "At first I thought I was going to be sick." He ran his fingers through his hair and told her about his visit with Tony.

Samantha was amazed at how easily he spoke about Tony. She wanted to wrap him in her arms and give him a big hug, but she didn't feel the timing was right. They hadn't seen each other in over a month, and now they were two people discussing a difficult time in his life.

"I'm glad you've mended your relationship with Tony. He loves you." *Do you love me?*

"Tony and Mary are family."

"Do you think he'll get years in jail for his crime?"

He stopped his pacing and looked at her. "He has to go through the formalities. Considering Vargas had kidnapped Mary and the captain did all he could to protect the witness, he'll be forced to retire and do community service for a few years. Jail time will be what he has already served."

"I'm glad. He's a good man who does anything to protect those he loves." Including taking a bullet for Nick.

Nick nodded in agreement. "You okay? I heard you've been chatting with the departmental shrink?"

"How did you hear that? That's a violation of my privacy." She jumped up, her temper rising.

"Don't get all shook up." He held up both hands in front of him, trying to calm her. "Some of the guys saw you going into her office a few times. Remember how the rumor got around about our RV trip?" She nodded. "Same grapevine at the precinct."

She sat back in her chair and relaxed. "You've heard a lot. Killing Vargas caused me some sleepless nights, but I'm doing better now." The therapist had also helped her to cope with her love for Nick, but she didn't want him to know about that part of her therapy.

"Taking a life is never easy."

"No. I still have terrible nightmares about that day, but they're fading." Not fast enough to suit her.

"Thank you for saving my life."

"I thought Vargas had killed you. He does in my nightmares. I'll never forget seeing him point his gun at you." Just mentioning it sent a chill through her.

He grabbed a chair and moved closer to her. She didn't budge. She needed to find out how he felt about her. She asked the question burning in her since his arrival. "Why did you come here?"

"I came to see if—" Nick stopped.

Why couldn't the man finish his sentence? He looked like he was choking on whatever he wanted to say. "If…?"

"Dammit." He pushed the chair away and knelt on the floor in front of her. Samantha leaned back in surprise. Nick grabbed her hand, kissed it, then blurted, "I love the hell out of you, Sam. Do you love me?

You'd better, because I can't stand to be away from you another minute. We're getting married right away. There. I said it." He caught a quick deep breath, and then let it out.

Samantha sat in her chair speechless. Was she dreaming? Nick wouldn't propose to her, a "rich" girl. Yet she dreamed of this day, longed for him to say those words, and even rehearsed a reply. Now the time was here and she couldn't utter a sound.

"Jeesh, Sam. Will you say something? I'm baring my soul here, and you decide to close your lips tighter than a clam at shucking time." His eyes pleaded with her for an answer.

"Yes, and yes," Samantha blurted out.

"Yes, what?"

"Yes, I love you with all my heart. Yes, I'll marry you whenever you say." She knew his reasons for a quick wedding, and she didn't want to delay being his wife for a second.

"You will?" He rose and took both of her hands in his, pulling her out of the chair. "Just like that? No arguments?"

His surprise tickled her. "None. And I won't run away." The look of gratitude, mixed with love in his eyes, brought those butterflies in her stomach to life once again. She could feel his tension. To relax him, she added, "It's about time you got your act together. I don't know how much longer I could have stopped myself from chasing after you."

"Yeah?" Nick put her hands on his chest and pulled her close by wrapping his strong arms around her waist. A giant smile brightened his face.

"And I don't chase," she replied as dignified as she

could manage with the warmth of his love flowing through her.

"Ah. But you do, my love. You chased my heart until you captured it. You're stuck with us forever."

"And you're stuck with mine." Samantha threw her arms around his neck and kissed him with all the pent up longing she possessed. At last, she was where she wanted to be—in the arms of her iron cop who would guard her body for a lifetime.

Samantha smiled to herself.

And do many, many other wonderful things to her, too.

She couldn't wait.

A word from the author...

A country girl at heart and the second of four children, I grew up on a small farm in upstate New York.

Working my way through college, I received a Bachelor's Degree in Business Education and a Master's Degree in Advanced Classroom Teaching.

Married to the love of my life, we raised three beautiful children. One of my greatest joys is being with my grandchildren.

I enjoy reading (romances of course), crocheting, working with various crafts, and traveling to many different regions of the world.

Belonging to the Romance Writers of America, Saratoga Romance Writers of America, New Jersey Romance Writers of America, and Mystery/Suspense Romance Writers of America have been a guiding light in my writing career.

Thank you for purchasing
this publication of The Wild Rose Press, Inc.

If you enjoyed the story, we would appreciate your
letting others know by leaving a review.

For other wonderful stories,
please visit our on-line bookstore at
www.thewildrosepress.com.

For questions or more information
contact us at
info@thewildrosepress.com.

The Wild Rose Press, Inc.
www.thewildrosepress.com

Stay current with The Wild Rose Press, Inc.

Like us on Facebook

https://www.facebook.com/TheWildRosePress

And Follow us on Twitter
https://twitter.com/WildRosePress